To my husband and family who tolerate me when my body is there, but my mind is elsewhere. I love you so much more.

A whimsically told tale full of adventure, Woodencloak's endearing troll princess heroine will enchant middle-grade readers as she plunges into peril and discovers how brave she truly is.

— CARRIE ANN NOBLE, AWARD-WINNING AUTHOR OF *THE MERMAID'S SISTER* AND *THE GOLD-SON*

Woodencloak is a delightful adventure that turns fairytales upside-down and redefines heroism. With engaging characters and fantastic worldbuilding, this is a story you'll delight in, no matter your age!

— AVILY JEROME, HAVOK EDITOR AND AUTHOR OF *THE AMULET SAGA* SERIES AND *THE BREEDING*

Woodencloak

THE BAND OF UNLIKELY HEROES BOOK 1

DAWN FORD

Published by ScrivKids,
an imprint of Scrivenings Press LLC
15 Lucky Lane
Morrilton, Arkansas 72110
https://ScriveningsPress.com

Printed in the United States of America

Paperback ISBN 978-1-64917-268-6

eBook ISBN 978-1-64917-269-3

Editor: K. Banks

Cover by Linda Fulkerson, bookmarketinggraphics.com

ACKNOWLEDGMENTS

Above all else, I thank God for His everlasting patience with me and for giving me inspiration that ignites joy in my heart.

Next, I'm so thankful for my husband John, along with my kids and their spouses who are willing to listen to me and brainstorm when I'm stuck. You keep me on my path and going when I'm not sure I can read or type another word.

For all of my writing friends who support and cheer me on, especially my critique groups—I could not do this without your unfailing help.

To Janeen Ippolito. Thank you for sitting with me and untangling the snares and my own inadequacies that I can't see past. Your mentoring and writing advice are worth more than gold. You bow to no one, my friend.

Lastly to Linda, Erin, Kaci, and all of the Scrivenings family, I'm so incredibly thankful for you all. I can't think of another group I'd rather work with and walk this publishing journey with than you.

CHAPTER I

Horra Fyd hunched forward on her granite throne, her bottom numb from sitting so long. The starched lace on her collar poked her troll earlobes.

"Sit up!" Horra's royal instructor, Woodsly, hissed at her.

King Divitri, Horra's father, slid a glance at her from atop his high-backed quartz throne.

Horra squirmed under her father's intense perusal. Anyone who didn't know the king wouldn't catch the tic in his cheek, a giveaway to his displeasure. Horra, however, knew it by heart. An urge to sigh grew, but she stifled it.

Her hobgoblin maid had chosen a dress of pure, stiff torture for Oddar's weekly Goblin Court. If sitting through hours of trivial arguments weren't uncomfortable enough, her dress tipped the scales.

"Tailfeathers," she muttered low enough that her father wouldn't hear.

Woodsly, however, did. He made a note on his parchment.

Vinegar! The rigid fabric prickled her neck.

Her royal troll schoolmates sat on the opposite side of the thrones in the galley. They got away with passing notes and whispering.

Horra ignored them and turned to listen to a group of shopkeepers requesting aid for a sudden pest invasion.

Boring! Horra's attention waned.

"How close are we to the end?" Her father's voice boomed, making the gulpy heralds jump. Their overlarge heads atop scrawny bodies bobbed to and fro furiously. It was almost entertaining enough to take Horra's mind off her stiff dress.

Horra shifted as her collar poked again. *Stupid recapper laundresses!* Always using prickly powder in the wash to get back at her because she was messy.

When she turned sixteen and became Queen of Oddar, she would outlaw prickly powder in the royal laundry soap. There were many things she would outlaw, including long, boring Goblin Courts.

A high-ranking messenger stepped in the center of the aisle, clicked his tongue, and smacked his fist against his chest in salute. "Queen Stella Toppenbottom of the Fairy Overkingdom has requested an audience with your Majesty."

Not another royal meeting! This was going to make an already unbearable day longer. Besides, what in the world brought a fairy queen across the Wilden Lands to Oddar? Fairies never visited them. Had a troll stuck a warty toe on their glittering land?

Her father nodded. "Let her come."

The messenger stepped back and bowed.

Two of Oddar's mightiest trolls pulled the iron rings set in the carved, marble doors. They creaked heavily, and rock dust whirled to the floor as they opened.

Six graceful male fairy guards strutted in, their diaphanous wings twitching. Waning light rays shifted, coalescing into a haloed spotlight as a regal woman stepped across the threshold. Gold, shimmering fabric danced around her nimble body. Her crystal slippers crunched against the rubble on the floor. A diamond tiara sat upon her white-blonde head, and she held a bejeweled scepter topped with a pearl globe. Her iridescent wings fluttered softly at her back.

The fairy queen! Horra recalled her mother, who loved telling scary stories, reading about fairies. They were pretty and fluttery and irresistible to most creatures. The fairy's ability to bewitch gave Horra nightmares as a young troll. She shook the memories off.

Behind the regal fairy glided two equally grandiose girls. They both wore silky pink dresses and silver heels. A blonde wore a pale pink gown with floral trim. The other, a brunette, wore a darker pink gown with ivy trim. Their crowns and wings weren't as pronounced as the queen's, but there was no doubt these were fairy princesses.

Horra slid a glimpse across the royal peerage. The male trolls' gazes were drawn to the fairies, their eyes wide and enthralled.

She contemplated what it was that was so unappealing about the creatures. There were so many things, from their shimmering wings to the delicate nature of their slim bodies. If one sneezed too hard, would they break in two? Explode into glitter, perhaps? Without their magic and beguilement, what could they do?

Her kind, with their dark green skin and brawny bodies, were built for hard work, fighting, and war. They were much more fierce than these gleaming creatures.

King Divitri nodded in deference. "Queen Toppenbottom, it is my honor to welcome you to Oddar. You've come a long way. How can I help you?"

The queen dipped her head. "King Fyd. Thank you for

welcoming our most unexpected visit. I'm afraid I come with dire news. Is it possible we have a private audience?"

Queen Toppenbottom's sweet voice jangled like wind chimes. It grated on Horra's patience. She turned from the effervescent light, which danced in happy circles around the fairies.

The Overkingdom sent so many complaints to Oddar that her father no longer responded to their beautiful scripts sent via whimsy bird messengers. Possibly, the fairies had grown tired of their birds not returning and their messages being ignored.

Every male eye of the Goblin Court, down to the youngest heralds, was riveted to the fairies. Annoyed, Horra shifted away to a view of Skog Marsh out a side window.

Woodsly tapped his quill on the parchment. Of all creatures in the room oblivious to fairies' charm, it had to be her woodgoblin instructor! His bark was thicker than she'd realized.

Horra sat up straighter but kept her glimpse of the marsh. It was almost time for the bog bogies' croaking song. She loved falling asleep to their melodies.

Woodsly cleared his throat, an obnoxious *clackity* sound, which, though quite normal for a woodgoblin to make, disturbed her troll senses. A fact Woodsly knew full well.

Horra reluctantly glanced at him.

He frowned at her.

She frowned back and twisted to gaze through the window once more.

The air was full of overripe sweetsuckle flowers coming off of the fairies in waves. It assaulted her nose. She ground her teeth together to keep from sneezing. Her ear twitched at the stiff collar again. She made plans to burn the dress when she got back to her bedchambers. *IF* she ever got back to her bedchambers.

Jingling laughter echoed across the chamber.

Oh, bother! She was forgetting her manners. Horra pasted her social smile back on and turned toward the princesses.

A head taller than any creature present, an ambassador's son and her classmate, Torren chuckled at her before following their classmates out of the courtroom. She narrowed her eyes and glared back. He knew how much Horra loathed performing formal duties and teased her endlessly about it.

"Are you finished daydreaming?" Woodsly clacked, startling her.

Vinegar! Would she ever be free of her tutor's disapproval?

She was surprised to realize her father and the queen were gone. How long had she been distracted?

The princesses leaned into each other, a flurry of warring pinks, their tinkling voices a tittering mish-mash she couldn't make out. They reminded her of the beautiful fizzbugs that invaded the swamp in an epidemic of colorful wings during the spring and fall seasons. She had a board in the lab with dozens of them pinned to it.

Behind them, the four remaining male fairies stood on alert with their arms by their sides and wings fluttering at their backs.

"Come. Let's show our honored guests around while your father and the queen meet."

Woodsly held the ladder so Horra could climb down from the throne. Though her chair was smaller than the King's, she was still short enough to need help descending.

Heat spread across her cheeks. Normally Woodsly honored her enough to wait until everyone dispersed from the throne room before producing the ladder. Obviously, her mud-headedness irritated him enough not to show her preference. "Show them where?"

She took his slim-limbed hands in her chubbier ones so she

could get down without turning around. For years she hadn't grown as normal trolls do, and Woodsly had left her hanging on the throne a time or two when she'd been too petulant.

Woodsly stepped back and folded his hands in front of him. "Princess Horra, where do we start a castle tour when we have royal guests?"

She ignored the stupid collar prickling her ear once more. Taking a deep breath, she straightened. "If you will please follow me."

CHAPTER 2

The fairy's footsteps crunched on the gritty floor while Horra pointed to statues and noble objects, and droned on with information she'd rehearse three times a week for two years of primary royal training.

They reached the side door to the Hall of Monstrosity. Hobgoblin servants dusting the numerous exhibits scurried out of their way murmuring things about the 'charmed ones.' Horra thanked the Creature God that her hide repelled fairy magic. It resisted most types of magic. Unfortunately, it had also kept magic from curing her mother.

Which was why magic wasn't good for much of anything.

The princesses dawdled behind, which was not an easy feat since Horra's legs were five times shorter than theirs. They remained close together, whispering back and forth, their male fairy escorts behind them.

What was with all the brooding? They'd not been summoned to Oddar. They'd even come without an invitation.

Horra renamed them Misery and Gloomy.

Shaking off her grim musings, she stepped up to the wall of portraits surrounding the chamber. She stood beside the stuffed head of the biggest swamp swine ever recorded and placed her claw on the massive tusk.

With her free hand, she tried to motion elegantly at the first picture and gave them her rehearsed speech on the historical queens and kings of Oddar.

She reached her mother's portrait, where she faltered. "This is my mother Terra's portrait. It is said she lived up to her name and was terrifying in battles. Similarly, my grandmother before her, Queen Petra, embodied her name during her reign."

"I thought Oddar was ruled by female trolls. Why is your father allowed to rule while you live?" the brunette fairy asked.

Horra wanted to ask why they cared since they seemed so bored, but etiquette dictated she not return insolence for insolence. She put some sigh into her exhaled breath. "Father is my proxy by a blood oath. As Queen's Champion, he rules in my place by Oddar law until I turn sixteen. Then he will step down into a Royal Advisor position after my coronation." She glanced at their blank faces. "It's all rather complicated."

Horra assumed since fairies had innate magic, an energy which pooled inside of their being, they wouldn't understand that as non-magical beings, trolls were subject to the magic of the land.

She returned her gaze to her mother's picture. Long ruby hair twisted in braids around her light green, warty hide. Red hair was a royal trait Horra had inherited. She smoothed a claw across her long tresses. Pride burst in her chest for their unruly, red manes—wild as their rugged spirits.

Queen Terra had been a mighty troll warrior. She'd beaten Horra's father in the Battle of the Bogs, a traditional troll competition. Her father used to joke that he fell for her mother in more than one way that day.

Horra both smiled and cringed a bit at the memory of her father's declaration of love. Once, her father had been able to laugh and show love. Her mother's death had locked him inside himself. And Horra no longer had a key.

Her biggest goal in life was to be as great a troll warrior as her mother and their foremothers before them. Horra turned to ask if her guests had any questions.

The fairy princesses stared in disinterest around the room. Their willowy daintiness was out of place amongst the troll's fierce portraits. Horra bit back a stinging comment. She wouldn't ever dishonor someone in this fashion, but she was Oddar's ambassador. There would be no marks on Woodsly's parchment for this.

"The next room is the Grand Library. Its walls are carved out of the rarest alabaster, which glows in the dark, allowing us to read even on the darkest nights. The outer wall is glassed and looks over Oddar's Iron Mountains, a rich view of the tallest mountains in all of the Wilden Lands, except for the elfin mountains, of course. Above the library, my foremothers built a maze of walkways instead of a ceiling because they believed learning has no limits. It's the biggest library in all of Trolldom. I believe we have a few fairy spellbooks—"

"Yes, spoils from the War of the Warts," the blonde fairy stated. Air pulsed around her carrying her displeasure. "Ill-gotten gains from a ridiculous war the fairies were tricked into signing on to. Those items should rightfully be on display in our Hall of Light to honor our fairy knights who died courageous deaths." Although the pretty princess's voice tinkled like bells, her words burned like a bungbee sting to Horra.

The other fairy nodded in agreement.

Were they kidding?

Horra's claws dug into her palms, and she opened her

mouth to set the fliffity fairies straight when Woodsly stepped in front of her. She was left with a view of his ridged tail sticking out of his bark suit coat. Not a pretty sight.

"Yes, well, as I'm sure you know, there are two sides to every tale. Especially when war is involved. Let's continue our tour with the Conservatory. I'm sure you'll find our unique gardens fascinating," Woodsly said.

Horra's fangs ground against her upper teeth. She took the moment hidden behind her instructor's trunk to regain her composure. When Woodsly turned toward her and held out an arm to allow her lead, she found some solace in the glimmer of irritation in his gray eyes. It was what she needed for strength to replace her royal poise.

Sunlight was quickly turning to dusk, so Horra snapped her flint-like nails to light the torches lining the cavern walls along the back of the castle to the Conservatory. Normally Horra, with her night vision eyesight, wouldn't use the torches, but just last week she'd read in *Beasties: An Instruction Guide,* that fairies didn't have the same capacity for night vision. And she didn't want them wondering off dark corridors unattended.

"Mustn't start another War of the Warts," Horra murmured as she unlocked the Conservatory doors with a special key hung on the wall outside of the door. Some of the creatures they kept inside were smart enough to open unlocked doors.

"Imagine, using a key to open a door!" one of the princesses exclaimed behind her.

Horra spun around to face them. Her flesh heated with the implied insult. She should've known magic would be brought up.

The blonde fairy swiped away a spider web that was too high for their servants to reach. Too far up to bother Horra, the most frequent visitor to the room. "No more astonishing than the state of this castle. It would only take one good spell ..."

Chin raised, Horra snarled, "Trolls don't use shortcuts like magic to do what a being is quite capable of doing themselves. Hard work is the bounty—"

"Of a kingdom. Yes, so we've heard. You don't really believe that, do you?" Tinkling laughter from the brunette fairy carried an edge of derision.

Clattering came from Woodsly's throat again. "Your pardon, Majesties. That is Oddar's motto, just as 'Magic, Music, and Beauty Are Our Strength' is the Fairy Overkingdom's motto. I'm sure you wouldn't like others bashing your ideals whilst in your castle, hmm?" Woodsly's smile was as wooden as Horra had ever seen it, and that was saying something for a woodgoblin.

"If you'd like, I can return you to the entry to wait for your mother, the queen." A grin fought to be loosed at the possibility of dropping the spoiled fairies off in the outer room full of gremlins and imps vying to have the king hear their grievances.

A look of repulsion crossed both princesses' faces.

Horra turned and pushed the Conservatory's glass doors open. The scents of moss and muck thickened the air. She drew in a deep, aromatic breath. The neckline pricked her ear again, reminding her she couldn't get her dress dirty or the redcappers would use more prickly powder in the next washing.

Inside, a metal-webbed frame held up the glassed-in walls and ceiling. Bog bogies croaked in the distance from a troll-made pond. Pygmy clodhoppers creaked from their holes in the dirt. This was her sanctuary.

An enormous pudge wudgie flapped from the limbs of a wicked willow tree and soared across the grand expanse of the Conservatory.

It flew directly at the princesses, claws out.

The fairies screamed.

Horra giggled.

Sparkles erupted in the air where the princesses had just stood.

CHAPTER 3

It was the most horrifying aspect of Horra's mother's fairy tales: fairies could disappear at will, leaving behind a pile of fairy dust. It never failed to make Horra's hide crawl, but seeing it in real life was much worse. Goosebumps bloomed across Horra's arms and legs and settled into a sickening ball in her stomach.

"What is that monstrosity?" screeched a disembodied voice. A second later, more sparks exploded. The fairies returned to their corporeal forms. Both of their brows were furrowed and their lips puckered.

The wudgie stood as tall as Horra unless she counted the long feather bobbing on top of its head, which floated up to the chins of the fairies. Pidge's feathers, black as a tar pit, gleamed in the moonlight like spilled oil. Her claws clicked on the stone terrace as she fluffed her feathers.

It screeched and nudged Horra's hand. She usually carried minced mice in her pockets. "Not now, girl. I'll bring you a snack later."

Horra turned toward their guests, anxious to introduce her

favorite pet. "This is Pidge. I raised her from an egg." She stroked Pidge's soft head and spoke in a low voice so as not to excite her. "Pudge wudgies are extremely rare, you know. Their ebony beaks catch a great price on the underground market. I've made it one of my missions to save their species."

"They're hunted for good reason. They're vicious." The brunette fairy held her nose, so the tinkling voice sounded more like a broken chain now. It suited her far more than the annoying chime-like sound it had been.

Pidge glared at the fairies with wide golden eyes as if she understood their words. She snapped her beak and screeched, and the fairies squealed in reply.

The male fairies moved in front of the princesses protectively.

"Pidge will attack if you act scared. But we know there's nothing to be afraid of, right?" Horra scratched the wudgie's neck to distract her from the sugar-coated princesses.

"Beg your pardon, but I'd keep that beast under control. One scratch and my queen will insist you get rid of it," a male fairy spoke through tight lips.

The wudgie screeched and hobbled across the stones until she could spread her wings to fly back to her nest.

Horra turned toward the male fairy. "This is a sanctuary. Fairies have no dominion here."

"Can we go back, now? I'm feeling a bit ill." The blonde fairy was flushed a bright pink, matching her gown, and not at all becoming.

She'd look better in a shade of green.

Woodsly cleared his throat, which made the blonde turn crimson. He tapped his quill against the parchment. "Princess Horra. Perhaps it's time to go."

Weariness weighed on Horra's shoulders. It'd been a long

day, and she'd looked forward to spending time here. But it was obvious fairies and pudge wudgies didn't mix.

Horra reluctantly turned away from the lush gardens. The stiff collar poked, and her ear twitched again. Though her troll hide was thick, the spot wore thin. Soon she'd have a blister.

"Come along, then. It's time for the evening meal. I believe the cook is preparing goose liver gruel tonight. It's not my favorite, but bitter grog eases the greasy aftertaste."

Both princesses gagged, then the blonde fainted dead away on top of a thorny henbane bush.

The male fairies were there in an instant to catch her, but it was too late. The thorns sliced through the dress like butter, and silver blood seeped through the gown.

Horra rushed with her arms out. Oh, no! No matter what she thought of them, one of the fairies getting hurt would be a disaster to handle. She was stopped short by a fairy guard who stepped between her and the princess.

The second guard produced a bottle, uncorked it, and poured it on the wounds. The blood dissipated and the dress stitched itself back together.

"What was that?" Horra asked, stepping around the first guard in surprise. She loved potions and ointments, it was her favorite subject. She reached out to touch it.

A sword materialized in the hand of the male fairy blocking her, grazing her nose, and making it itch. "Stand back. No one touches the princess."

A hobgoblin stepped through the Conservatory's doors and thumped a fist to his chest, then bowed. "Dinner is served."

The blonde fairy swooned again.

Horra rolled her eyes and ushered them out before anyone got injured.

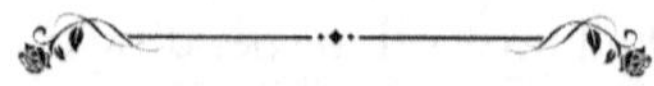

ANNOYING, tinkling music filled the dining room where tables overflowed with food. Roast swamp swine, turnips au gratin, garlic three-weed salad, and two of Horra's favorite condiments —horseradish relish and beet-juice cocktail—adorned the marble table top. No gruel. This was a feast of special preparation, and the metal trays and plates all gleamed beneath a chain-suspended candle chandelier.

Horra was certain the hobgoblins must've worked double-time to accommodate their unexpected guests.

Horra's mouth watered as she walked to her chair. However, the queen was seated in it. King Divitri didn't notice Horra's confusion since he was in a deep discussion with the royal fairy.

She couldn't imagine anything a fairy said could be nearly that interesting. "Father?" she asked.

He waved a hand as if to dismiss her, not even looking her way.

Her throat tightened as she held back the sting of the slight. The king wasn't overly affectionate, but he also didn't ignore her in public, either. This wasn't like him at all. However, the two opposing royals were quite oblivious to her presence.

Horra turned around to ask Woodsly where to sit, but he was no longer behind her. She hesitated. Except in the Conservatory and the swamp, she was always told where to go and what to do. She was at a loss.

Not so the fairies. They were all seated by the time Horra caught her wits and walked to where the last empty seat remained—at the far end of the table by the male fairy who had pulled a sword on her.

Vinegar! Woodsly must've been called away when she wasn't looking. Now who would she talk to?

A hobgoblin servant placed Horra's steps by the chair. She could almost feel everyone watching as she climbed into it, especially Torren, who loved to tease her about 'the weather down there' or any other of his incessant digs at her size.

A glance his way assured her, though, that Torren's attention was focused on a fairy princess alone. Hmph! That was why female trolls made better rulers.

Horra bowed her head for grace, but no grace was uttered as per usual. The fairies dug into the food with astounding speed. She frowned at their manners and again at the twinkling notes of the music that had been playing since she'd entered the room. No musicians cluttered the corners as they did at the holiday balls. There were no instruments at all.

Was it fairy magic? It was all tinkly-sounding, like the fairies. She turned around, trying to locate the origin of the magic with no luck.

The first platter to pass by her had one spoonful of three-weed salad left. Her beet juice was "accidentally" taken by the male fairy next to her, who apologized but didn't offer her his glass. In front of them, the decanter was already empty. She signaled the hobgoblin servant, who was stopped on the way by the brunette princess. The hobgoblin turned and headed back toward the kitchen.

Each of the next platters came to her empty. She glanced around the table. The fairy's plates were not that full. Neither were any of the royal troll's plates. The table had been loaded with food enough for twice as many as were now present. How had the food disappeared so quickly?

At least the roast was only half gone. Just one more fairy to go before her turn. She searched again for the hobgoblin servants to signal that she needed more beet juice, but they were missing.

The platter of swamp swine was finally passed to her. All

that was left was the snout, the hooves, and some juice around the bones of the beast.

She turned a suspicious eye toward the male fairy. She glimpsed a grin as he wiped his mouth.

Horra slammed her fork down on the table. All talking ceased and everyone turned to stare at her.

Her father frowned and blinked as if just awoken from a dream. "Is there something wrong, daughter?"

"May I please be excused? I'm full." She held up the last platter to show him.

His cheek ticced. No doubt he'd think she ate it all.

"Fine, you're dismissed. But we'll discuss your eating habits later." King Divitri's words were slurred slightly, and Horra wondered how many spiked beet juices he'd ingested already.

Horra sneered at the too-satisfied male fairy and climbed down the steps with as much dignity as possible.

She pushed the dining-room door open and strode through. Before she could close it, it slammed shut behind her.

CHAPTER 4

Horra hurried to her room, tore the dress off, and flung it into the fireplace. The flames crackled and turned purple from the prickly powder, reflecting on the unmined gems in the walls. In an instant, the dress was ashes.

Tears leaked out of her eyes and she swiped them away with a careless hand, scratching herself with a sharp claw. "What a stupid day!" she shouted at the flames.

It wasn't enough. She kicked, and her proper shoes tumbled across the floor. She stretched her feet and wiggled her toes. Her ear was sore from the collar, but she had no ointment. With her thick hide, she rarely needed any kind of first aid. "Stupid fairies with their stupid ointments."

Her stomach gurgled. She hadn't had lunch and had only managed to grab a chunk of bracken bread, without the bacon grease, for breakfast. Today had been chock-full of cases for the Goblin Court before the fairies had arrived.

Horra changed into a new pair of pants and, since tomorrow was wash day and everything else was dirty, the last shirt in her dresser—a wrinkled tunic. After pushing her secret code into the jewels near her bed, a square stone panel shifted and opened up, revealing a secret passage that ran through the castle.

The walls in the passageway were void of any of the gems, having been mined years ago and used by her foremothers to finance the building of the castle around the passages. Because of this, the gray walls were pocked and uneven in all but a few of the walls. Rock bits and dust gathered everywhere and her feet ground against the grit as she stepped inside.

She took a deep, cleansing breath and sealed the panel behind her, and headed down the passage toward the kitchen. Relief rushed through her at being in her hidden space, a place no fairy would ever find, and she grinned.

She'd get something to eat, even if it was swampfruit, and find out what the fairies had done to the servants that made them leave and not come back. And then maybe she'd be able to bribe one of the hobgoblins for information about why the fairies came all this way to meet with her father and how long they planned to stay—hopefully only until after supper was finished. They could travel home faster by fairy paths, after all. They wouldn't need to stay in the castle even for nightfall.

That thought cheered her somewhat.

A few yards from her bedroom, Horra realized rats were sitting up on their haunches, swaying back and forth. Though she often witnessed vermin along the passages, this was an unusual amount of them, and they were acting strangely.

She stopped to study them, curious about their odd, dazed motion. Were they diseased? There wasn't any kind of frothing coming from their mouths. They ranged in all sizes and colors. She hunched over to look at them, her claws digging into her thighs as she considered.

A particularly large one let out a half-squeak, half-growl. It didn't flinch when she waved a hand in front of its face.

She wrinkled her nose. "What in the Wilden Lands? Has this whole castle gone crazy?"

At the sound of her voice, the dazed rats dropped to the ground and like rubber balls, bouncing from wall to wall before disappearing.

Horra shook her head. "Magic. That's what it is. Worse than poison. Maybe Woodsly will let me do some sort of experiment with mice and fairy dust." He enjoyed giving Horra extra homework, especially anything that involved the lab. It was tedious work, but she loved working there the most.

Her stomach grumbled once more, and she dismissed the mice and the fairies from her mind. She needed food! She hurried through the maze of secret passages to the kitchen.

Down the hallway to her right, she could smell the smoky scents from the woodstove. Her stomach twisted in expectation. A lever along the passage wall opened a shelf into a storage room used for grains and vegetables in the dark back corner. Since meal preparation for the day would be over, she could slip in and out without fear of being caught.

The panel scraped against the floor to close behind her. A jar of snake oil on the shelf tipped over the edge as it closed. The jar slipped in her fingers, but Horra caught it and set it back on the shelf. She wiped the greasy residue off on her tunic as she walked across the room to the door that opened into the kitchen.

Hobgoblins rushed around, which was odd. Even with their fluffity guests, they should be finishing their cleaning at this hour. She tried to catch the attention of several, but none of them paid her any mind.

Her mother had been right about fairies. They were particularly awful to have around.

There was one servant, an older hobgoblin standing back against the wall. Horra grabbed her arm. "Excuse me, but what is going on?"

The woman turned toward her with wide eyes. She shook her head and pointed to her ears. "I can't hear you. Dropped my hearing aid. I don't understand what's going on."

Horra pointed to the others racing around like the rats in the passageway and held her arms up indicating she was just as confused.

As if on silent cue, those servants gathered their trays, bowls, and pitchers and marched in single file from the kitchen into the hallway that led to the dining room.

Horra stepped out of their way and pulled the deaf servant with her. No wonder the hobgoblins avoided the fairies. She shivered at the thought of having her mind controlled like that. She'd discuss their horrid behavior with her father in the morning, though it might not do any good since it fell under diplomacy. Still, she'd not hesitate to tell him what she thought.

Her stomach gurgled again. The older servant appeared bewildered and shuffled back away from everything.

Horra caught her attention, pointing at the icebox. She was almost starving and wanted to get something before the other servants returned. "I'm going to get some food." She motioned like she was eating.

The servant scratched at her graying bun of hair, nodded, and walked out of the castle. Was she confused or lost? Perhaps the woman was getting too old to serve? Another thing she'd have to take up with the king tomorrow.

Across the kitchen, Horra opened the icebox to grab whatever she could to take back to her room and eat while reflecting on the strange events of the evening.

The stuffed toadstools were slimy now that they'd cooled, but she popped them into her mouth as she shuffled through the leftovers. The beet juice was sour, and she was thirstier than she realized. Half the jug was gone before she took a breath.

She continued to rummage. Ah-ha! There, in the back, was a hunk of roast swamp swine, hidden behind the pokeweed berry parfait. The tangy scent of the pokeweed berries was almost enough to tempt her to dip a claw in, but a rattle echoed down the hallway, catching her attention.

It sounded like Woodsly's warning whistle. The last time he'd used it was on the archery green when an errant arrow flew straight for her head. She was sure it had been Torren trying to throw her off her game. However, had she not reacted quickly, she could've been killed.

The whistle was never a false alarm.

Horra hesitated, heart racing, and glanced around. She spied no danger. Hunger drove her to take one last, big bite of the roast before she shoved it back on the shelf. She swiped a hand across her mouth to clean the grease away.

Her pointed ears pricked at the sound of her father's shouts. He growled in pain. What was going on? If it hadn't been for Woodsly's whistle, she might have dismissed her father's shouts as temper and too much drink.

Together, however?

Fear squeezed her heart. What had she been taught in defense class? Grab the nearest weapon, whatever there might be, and face your opponent fearlessly. She grabbed a butcher knife, which hung on the wall beside the hearth. Her father's yell became muffled and unintelligible.

Horra raced down the servants' hallway.

The dining hall was in chaos. Platters were overturned and plates were in pieces across the stone floor. Hobgoblins darted around, gathering the debris into tablecloths. All of the guests were gone.

But the tinkling music remained.

She clutched the butcher knife in the air in one hand, but she didn't see any threat. The hair on her neck rose when she spied the royal rug which always laid beneath her father's chair wrinkled and dragged toward the door on the other side of the room.

"Father!" She moved toward the door. Where were the fairies? Where were the guests? She turned to question a frantic hobgoblin about the rug when another door banged open.

Woodsly stumbled in. The whistle he kept neatly hidden under his wooden collar was broken and dangling from his neck. His terrified glance jerked around the room until he caught sight of her. He collapsed to the floor and wheezed, "They've all been taken. The king ... gone. Run, Horra! Hide! Save yourself!"

Woodsly's body shimmered. His bark changed from a lively silver to a dead gray, drying and cracking as though aging before her eyes. Finally, the husk of his body lay unmoving, his bark shed, leaving a slim trunk and limbs behind. His fingers were replaced by leaves that bloomed, then shriveled, and then died. In the blink of an eye, her instructor was nothing more than kindling.

The butcher knife clanged to the ground at her feet.

CHAPTER 5

A chunk of bark at the heart of the lifeless limb fell, revealing a glowing seed with a leaf sticking out of it. The nut gleamed dark brown.

Disbelief rocked her. Shock stole her breath and her ears rang as she struggled to grasp what had just happened. It couldn't be!

But it was. This wasn't a training exercise.

She knew the legends. Woodsly always made sure she learned her history. When a woodgoblin's life ended, they could choose to pass on to the next life or regenerate using their life essence. But it was difficult at best, and they had to reach sacred soil in the Weald to be replanted for that new life to take hold and grow.

Chills raced across Horra's warty hide. All noise ceased as if time stood still. The seed rolled across the floor and stopped at her claws. She stared at it. Tightness gripped her chest.

"It's up to you now, Princess. You're our only hope. Fulfill your destiny." The words spoken in her mind were Woodsly's. She could smell him—wood chips and polish.

But that made no sense because her instructor was no longer alive.

She blinked. Sound exploded around her, and the shock was gone. None of it made sense, but she knew she had to move. Her mother, who had survived the War of the Warts as a young troll, always ensured she was trained on the possibility of someone invading the castle. Her mother's instructions flew to the front of her mind: *"Run to the passageways, my darling girl. Lock them up tight and you'll be safe there. Never let anyone know about them. Your life might depend upon it."*

Horra grabbed the nut and hustled back toward the kitchen. But she was so slow. Hobgoblins clamored around her, blocking her way, their eyes glazed and unseeing.

Fear lodged in her gut as the tinkling music changed to low notes. Magic thickened around her. It was like slogging through the muddy mire in the swamp as she made her way against the magic's pull and past the mindless servants. It beckoned to her, calling for her to turn around and come. Sweat dotted her brow as she resisted. The pull turned into pain, and she struggled to get one foot in front of the other.

Cursed magic! It wasn't supposed to work on trolls. At least, it hadn't on her mother. Queen Terra's face crossed her mind's eye, and the spell broke.

Horra slid on roast juice in front of the icebox and tumbled to the floor. Unnatural power, heavy enough to hinder breathing, stole her air. Out of sheer panic, Horra crawled toward the storage room. Her sharp-clawed nails dug into the floor, propelling her along. She grabbed for the doorway, but an invisible force wrapped around her legs.

A discordant note rang into silence. Horra lay on the floor, unable to move.

A tall figure enshrouded in a black cloak entered the

kitchen from the dining room door. His bony hands were fisted as if holding something, but there was nothing there. "Magic is stronger than muscle, Princess, as your father just found out." He *tsked*. "If you come along willingly, it won't hurt at all."

Horra didn't recognize his voice. It had a booming quality, though he didn't speak loudly. Her head ached as if something pressed on it.

Behind the figure crept the old deaf hobgoblin, clutching a heavy frying pan. She swung it and smacked the cloaked person on his back. His head cracked on the thick, butcher-block table as he fell, and he crumpled to a heap on the floor. The pressure on Horra's legs and head dissolved.

The hobgoblin tapped her chest with a fist. "It's a coup. Run. I'll hold them off as long as I can, Princess."

Horra dashed into the storage room and across it to the shelf, jabbing the hidden release. She held her breath while the door opened slowly ... so slowly, and then closed equally as slow. She leaned against the stone passage wall.

What had just happened?

Usually, magic didn't work on trolls. It was why they afforded civil relations with the fairies when other races wouldn't. But that was no fairy. And what was with the music?

She shook her head, thankful the deaf hobgoblin servant had come back when she did. She'd have to find a way to reward her.

"Where did she go?" The male fairy's voice, which she recognized from the Conservatory, was unmistakable.

"I believe I saw her run outside, sir," came the voice of the old hobgoblin.

Could the servant hear now? Or was she smart enough to cover for Horra?

"Nonsense. I would've felt the cold night's air if she had.

Trolls don't just disappear. She has to be here somewhere. Get a torch. I can't see anything in this room!"

Why did they want her? The hobgoblin mentioned a coup. She realized with a start it was because she was the rightful heir to the throne. The crown passed from mother to daughter. Her father was king on parchment only, sealed by laws a hundred years old. It *was* a coup like the War of the Warts, only this time, it was a more direct approach.

"Search for her! Turn every barrel over. Slash open every bag. I don't care what you do, but find her." It was the fairy queen's voice now, but it was no longer smooth and tinkly.

Horra glanced at the iron pin used to lock the secret panels. She'd never had to secure them because she'd never needed to. Her mother had—during the War of the Warts, while her mother, Queen Petra, had fought a dark mage who had sent the withering wart plague on all of the Wilden Lands. The Erlking.

They'd used the panels then. Iron, because magic wouldn't penetrate them. Too heavy for hobgoblins to lift, and fairies couldn't touch them without being poisoned.

Cobwebs and dust coated the pin that fit across the stone block to keep it from opening in case someone accidentally found the release trigger. Horra hefted the pin up, troll-strong despite her small stature. Even with her strength, the pin was long and weighty. Horra shakily slid it into the eye of the lock on the other side of the panel as quietly as possible.

A series of crashes sounded from the other side of the wall: shelves breaking, jars shattering. Her heart thudded hard in her chest, and though she didn't think anyone on the other side could hear, she struggled to control her labored breathing.

What did they want with Oddar? Her father? Her? The questions flew through her mind as she raced as fast as she could go back down the passage. She grimaced as her feet scrunched on rock debris along the carved stone path. She'd never gotten caught before, but this time was different. It wasn't just a mark on Woodsly's parchment at stake.

More questions popped up. Could it be fairy retribution for a generation-old war they'd signed on to because the plague of the warts had hit their shining kingdom particularly hard? Still, fairies weren't fighters in the battle sense. They were schemers and manipulators. So many, both trolls and fairies, as well as other creatures, had died. If it were revenge, why now?

The fairies' questions about troll matriarchy came back to her. Could it be because her claim to the throne wasn't binding yet? Trolls were vulnerable until she became queen and sealed the blessing of the Creature God to her reign.

Her father was susceptible because of it, weakened the past three years due to grief over losing her mother. Though he took the vows, he'd been a reluctant ruler. She'd never considered it before this moment. He'd pledged himself in marriage to her mother, who was bound to the kingdom by a blood oath to protect and keep it. Having been the only solo king ruler in Oddar's history, he hadn't taken a blood oath. A vow was strong, but not as strong as a blood oath.

No one had advised against it. Their advisors had all encouraged her father. Except for Woodsly, who had cautioned them, but hadn't stopped the ceremony. Horra thought him haughty at the time. He had been a tough tutor, legalistic in his training.

Her breathing echoed the rhythm of her footfalls, fast and heavy. Had Woodsly been working on the assumption something would happen before she turned sixteen, the ruling age? He was too smart not to. And he'd come to her in his final moments. She had to live up to his expectations.

Tears burned the backs of her eyes. She squared her back.

There was no time for fear and pity. With the memory of her mother's lessons on what to do in an emergency bolstering her resolve, she strengthened her stride. She needed to secure the other hidden passageways until she could figure out what in the name of dragon's fire was going on for sure.

CHAPTER 6

Had the passageway always been this long? Her legs strained against her determination to make them move faster. She skidded to a stop at each door, lifted the pins into the locks, and moved on. It took forever before she made it back to the stone panel by her room.

She dropped to the passageway floor, panting and exhausted. Grime coated her sweaty body, and cobwebs her hair. There was no telltale movement of vermin scurrying along. No sounds filtered through the stone walls. Her claws quivered as she wiped her moist brow.

If only she could get to the Armory, she could get some weapons. She longed for her bow and arrow, but she wanted—no, needed—more. Though she had been trained by Woodsly to be 'worthy of the calling of Queen,' as he'd so eloquently told her more times than she could count, the desire for someone else to be in charge overwhelmed her. She needed someone else to tell her what to do. But there wasn't anyone.

Tears seeped out of her pinched eyes. There was no holding them back. It was the first time since her mother died that she'd cried, and for a moment she didn't think she'd be able to stop. Her nose was runny when she finally managed to gain control over herself. She swiped a dirty sleeve across her swollen eyes and her running nose.

The only comfort she could have would be in figuring out what happened to her father and everyone else. She pulled the seed out from her pants pocket and studied it. It emitted a radiant light, the curled-up leaf already unfurling. "What would you instruct me to do now, Woodsly?"

Horra could almost hear his voice in her head telling her, "Chin up, you've important plans to make," and "Don't forget your shoes! Even warriors use footwear." She sighed. Her battle-readiness lessons hadn't covered what to do if her father was taken—possibly murdered—and her castle invaded.

"Think, Horra, think!" She tapped a claw against her temple to stave off a headache. Nose still runny, she sniffed and sighed. "Out. I need to find a way out."

She diagramed a crude map of the castle grounds on the dusty floor. "There are four ways out of the castle. One: I can go through my bedroom and try to sneak through the castle. My luck I'd run into one of them. But if I'm careful I won't. Two: The Conservatory has a hole in the wall I've used before to escape unseen."

Images of the fairies in her beloved Conservatory gave her pause. The male fairy said their queen would destroy the pudge wudgie because the bird was dangerous. Horra had found the egg when she was ten years old on a trip with her mother. The last trip they'd taken before she died.

They'd traveled to Norrow Lake, a mystical place that granted wishes to anyone lucky enough to find it. Horra wished for a pet. Her mother wished to be healed. The lake granted Horra's wish while declining her mother's. It had proved to her how heartless magic truly was. When they'd returned, Pidge had hatched the day her mother died.

There was no way anyone would harm a feather on that bird's head. She wouldn't let them.

"Option three: the dungeons beneath the castle have a chute that empties into the Scummut River." But she didn't fancy swimming through sewer water with its filth if she could help it.

"Or four: the kitchens. Definitely not safe." She pictured the hooded man and the spellbound hobgoblins.

"My room first. Then the Conservatory." Satisfied with having devised a plan, Horra crept to a spot by the fireplace where she'd picked a peekhole to check in case anyone was looking for her. Brusque words floated in the air, but the room was empty.

The nut jumped in her pocket. Horra dug it out and it slipped to the floor. "Woodsly, is that you?" The seed jittered left and then right. She frowned. "You need to conserve whatever magic you have left, or you won't grow."

The seed bumped into her clawed toe, almost as if he still scolded her in his infant stage. "Well, maybe if I were a nut, I'd understand what you were saying. Now pipe down or I'm feeding you to Pidge." She picked him up and put him in her pocket.

Back at the panel, she breathed deep before pulling the release lever. It whooshed open silently. She dug out from beneath her bed a knapsack that she used for hikes. It held many necessary survival items already, including a tent and sleeping bag. Along with everything she already had packed in the sack, she tossed clothes, a jeweled dagger—which had been her mother's—a smooth, marble compass, and a jar of pickled torentula eggs for Pidge.

Horra put on her hiking boots, and after a second of consideration added a pair of socks to the sack. She donned a jacket made from vapid vestra hide, a camouflaging fabric—another gift from Woodsly so she was 'prepared.' She apologized mentally for every time she'd groused when her instructor had insisted she be ready in case of a calamity. Her heart skipped a beat, and she checked her pocket to make sure the seed was safe.

Horra glanced around the room. She didn't think she needed anything else, so she moved over to her door to see if the hallway was clear. The music got louder the closer she stepped. It clanged with discordant notes in her ears, flatter than before. Voices rang down the hallway, so she dashed to the other side of the room.

Quickly, she pushed the jewels to enter the secret passageway with her bundle. The sack was heavier than she anticipated, but she hurried through and shut the panel behind her, locking it. She rushed to the peephole. The fairy queen swept into her room followed by the tall, hooded stranger. She spied a strange instrument resembling a pan flute in the stranger's hands. They glanced around the room and left.

With determined footsteps, she headed toward the Conservatory. "Please be there, Pidge."

The passage by the garden's panel was bathed in moonlight streaming down from the chapel's high glass windows. The only room on the third floor of the castle, it was inaccessible now. It had been her mother's favorite place to visit when she wasn't attending royal duties. Mother had said she was closer to the heavens and the Creature God there. Her father sealed the third-floor stairway off after her mother's funeral and forbade anyone from going in again. Luckily, her father was unaware of the secret passageways.

Horra traced the wall leading up to the window with her eyes. Having had no passage to get there, she'd tried to climb up the jagged wall once, but it'd been too high, and she'd gotten scared. Not unlike how she felt now. She braced herself and lifted the pin out. With a yank, the panel opened.

Silence.

No croaking bog bogies.

No chirping mudpiper's songs.

No breeze rifling through the swamp tree's leaves.

Horra's gut tightened. Had they been here already? She had to find Pidge.

The panel was set back behind a wall of creeping briar, a thorny vine known to cut to shreds anything that dared enter. She thanked the Creature God for her stunted size. Had she been any bigger, it would've been a struggle to get past the natural barrier, if she could do it at all. However, Horra knew where to crawl through where the barbs were less protrusive, the ivy more pliable, and the leaves glossier and easier to climb through.

Though a few thorns stuck to her back as she made her way out, she had no difficulty. Once through, she searched for danger before standing and whistling quietly for Pidge. At first, nothing—no rustle of leaves, no screeched greeting. Muted tinny music drifted through the walls. Her hands shook as she whistled as loud as she dared.

A tree rattled. Relief calmed her pulse some. Horra dug into the bag to get the jar of pickled torentula eggs. She whistled again and clicked her tongue. The tree quaked and a dark shadow glided across the garden.

The music grew louder. Horra had to hurry.

The eggs had a tangy, pungent scent. She tossed one in the air, and Pidge caught it. Unable to find a spot big enough to land, the large bird circled. Horra moved to a more open spot near the back of the garden. She whistled again and Pidge followed her.

Pidge landed beside Horra and nudged her arm for another treat. Horra tossed it to her, wanting to hurry, but not wanting to spook the bird. "Good girl. Let's go for a walk." She threw an egg every few steps to keep the pudge wudgie following her toward the hole in the wall. It was only twenty feet away but tricky to get to because it was hidden behind a gnarled, knotty tree.

Horra tripped over a root, and the jar tumbled away from her on the ground. Pidge instantly charged, gulping down the remaining eggs.

Vinegar! Now how was she supposed to get the bird to follow her?

Muted low notes resounded, and Horra was sure she caught someone talking—a fairy by the high-pitched sound of it.

"C'mon, girl. Follow me." She dredged some leaves through the pickle juice and held them up. Luckily the pickle scent was strong enough to keep Pidge's attention. If she could just get her pet a few more feet, they'd be free. The seed in her pocket wiggled and warmed.

"Woodsly, I promise I'm going to feed you to Pidge if you don't quit that!" her whisper sounded like a shout in the silence.

Pidge squealed for more treats. The door to the garden glowed with lanterns as the fairies and the hooded man entered. They stood in the same spot Horra and the princesses had earlier. All light from the moon shifted toward them, making her area more shadowed.

Horra's heart sunk to her belly. They'd found her.

CHAPTER 7

Horra tossed a wet leaf at Pidge. "Shh, follow me." She crept closer to the opening, around the weeping welter tree, and between the rope-like limbs that dangled around it. The fairies were talking, but she couldn't make out what they said. "This way, girl. Just a little bit further."

Pidge followed her. Her gleaming eyes focused on Horra's hands. She tossed the last leaf on the ground. They'd reached the gnarled tree. Pidge squealed again and nudged Horra's arm.

"Quiet!" she hissed. Her heart was going to burst from how hard it was beating. Sweat dampened her thick hair.

Circles of light burst into the air above them. Six piskies, miniature light fairies, buzzed around the trees, searching. Thankfully, the music had stopped.

Horra couldn't help the visions of pudge wudgie feathered purses and black-beak knives. It was the reason they were endangered. "C'mon girl." Horra tugged at Pidge's feathers but the bird snapped at her. Torentula eggs had probably been the wrong choice since they were Pidge's favorites. The seed jiggled in her pocket.

In frustration, Horra dug the nut out to admonish it again, but Pidge nipped at her fingers to get the seed. Horra held the glowing seed up and moved toward the hole. "We're almost there, girl. C'mon."

Shouts carried across the garden, calling her name. She reached the hole when plinking music filled the air. Pidge stopped and faced the direction the music came from. She bobbed her head, not unlike the rats in the passage. The air grew heavy.

Magic!

Horra yanked a long, ropey limb loose from the tree and tied a loop on the end. It wasn't as easy as the string she used to catch creatures in the swamp, but she'd done it hundreds of times. Her fingers twisted the pliable limb from memory. The magic notes changed and Pidge stepped away from her and toward the music. Horra fumbled with the final knot, and a salty streak of sweat dripped in her eye. In a flurry, she hooked the final twist and tossed it over Pidge's head right as the bird's wings unfurled.

"C'mon, girl. Don't listen to that racket!" Horra tugged on the rope-limb and dug her heels into the dirt as she pulled her pet toward the hole.

The music ended. "Horra, darling. Where are you? Your father is so worried about you." The queen fairy's voice, sweet and assuring.

Her father? For a second, Horra hesitated. The seed in her pocket heated enough to burn her. She swallowed a yelp and shook her head. *Lies. Fairy lies. That's all they were.*

She backed up, pulling on the rope to manipulate Pidge through the broken wall. They fell through the hole just as a piskie lit up the gnarled tree.

Horra plunged down the rocky mountainside, one hand holding her knapsack, the other holding the vine. Pidge's feathers tickled her as the bird toppled over her. Horra's head clipped a boulder and darkness took her.

When Horra opened her eyes, her skull throbbed, and several places stung with cuts and bruises from the fall. She was sprawled on a ledge of Nomans Mountain. She could see light glowing from the Conservatory windows above them. Something pecked at her. She jerked up, and Pidge, who was poised above her, squealed and jumped back.

"Sorry, girl. Thought you were a fairy." Fairies! That's right. She rubbed the sore spot on her head. They'd been about to escape the castle when they'd fallen out of the hole in the Conservatory's wall.

Pidge snorted and walked away. The rope limb dangled from her neck and dragged on the ground beside her.

Horra took in the area, her heart thundering with fear. She'd slipped out of the castle dozens of times, but she'd only ever gone down to the swamp. Though she could see in the dark, the mountain was different in the daytime. In the daylight, Horra would've known exactly where she was. And she knew this side of the mountain was dangerous angles, with jagged boulders and dizzying drop-offs.

A line of trees blocked her view of Skog Marsh. The leaf-covered limbs danced as synchronized, eerie shadows. She needed to get to the other side to make it to a clear path to the swamp where she could make her next plans.

What if the fairies were right behind them? She shook her head. Nah. They would've needed more piskies for that. She needed to move before daylight, though, or the fairies could sneak up on her.

Horra groaned as she rose. She wasn't out of shape, but she also hadn't exercised this hard in her life. She wondered about her father. Woodsly said he had been taken, but what did that mean exactly? Was he alive? Dead? She was torn. Could she leave without knowing his fate? The threat of getting caught by the cloaked man and the fairies was only too real. And then the seed would never get to the Weald.

She weighed the choices carefully in her mind like she'd been taught. There was only one thing she could do now. "First, the swamp, then the Weald," she told her pet. *If* she could find the elusive Weald. It didn't reveal itself to just anyone.

Pidge fluffed her feathers. Her golden eyes gleamed in the dark.

"Sorry I frightened you." Horra scratched the bird on its neck. She tried to loosen the rope, but it was tangled with stickery weed debris from their fall. She rubbed a hand over the pudge wudgie's body, trying to find an injury, but the bird didn't cry out in pain. There weren't any obvious wounds. "We need to get going, Pidge, or those fluffity fairies will get us."

Pidge bobbed her head as if in agreement before nudging her.

"I don't have any snacks, girl. You ate them all and then some." Horra tried to figure out where they were exactly. Trees and rocks covered the area surrounding them. From her position and the layout, this was the steep side of the mountain down from the library. How in the world did they get that far from the Conservatory's hole?

Pidge bumped her again and sat down next to her. The feather on top of her head quivered in the breeze as she eyed Horra sideways. She pecked at the rope, clasping it and dropping it on Horra's arm.

"What're you trying to tell me, girl?"

"She's tellin' you to get on her back." A bodiless voice

spoke. It was deep and gravelly, like a gnome's. Nope. It was a redcapper like the laundresses. Though only two to three feet in height, they were obstinate, treacherous, and vengeful, as proven with the prickly powder.

Horra's pulse sped. The dagger was inside the bag. There'd be no way of grabbing it if the creature attacked. "Who's there?"

"Who're you?" came the voice again. It wasn't as gruff as the first time. Probably eyeing her up to see if she had anything worth stealing. She could almost make out its hat in the bushes to her right.

Pidge nudged Horra's leg. The nut in her pocket thrashed. Horra backed up against Pidge and grasped the rope tight, shouldering the knapsack. If necessary, she'd drag the bird to safety.

Pidge moved, knocking Horra sideways. She flailed and grabbed hold of the rope and the feather on top of the bird's head.

In a whiff of wind, they were airborne. The feather Horra held snapped and her arm flopped. She grasped onto Pidge's neck feathers, leaving her dangling from the bird's side, clinging desperately to Pidge and the rope. The bird lurched higher and Horra screamed. She'd never been airborne before. Fear crippled her, and she couldn't move to adjust her hold. Her legs were too short to climb up on Pidge, so she hung on for life as the pudge wudgie flew.

Trees were shadows, and the moon was a white light in the sky as Pidge glided, and Horra hung. They flew through tall stringy pine trees, over a crest, and across the side of a different mountain. Pidge's feathers loosened and were carried in curling circles on the wind.

Horra's fear morphed, and she kicked her feet as if she

could gain traction to keep her hold. But there was nothing but cold night air.

She was going to fall.

CHAPTER 8

Pidge swooped downward. Her extensive wings stretched as she descended closer to the ground. More feathers loosened, and the pudge wudgie screeched.

Horra lost her grip completely and plummeted head over boots into a stream of frigid water. The sensation was a shock, and she lay immobile for an instant, the air knocked out of her. She gasped, and frigid water entered her nose and mouth. She thrashed around to get her head above the shallow stream.

Horra splashed, more floundering than swimming until she got her feet beneath her. She coughed out the water she'd ingested, which burned her nose and throat.

"Gah, Pidge. I hate cold baths." Even though she needed to wash off the cobwebbed grime from the passageways, she would've preferred anything to the icy stream. She teetered, slipping over slick rocks to the shore, dragging her knapsack and trying to calm her racing heart. Each time she thought she had it under control, another spasm of coughs racked her body, and it took several breaths to clear the water from her airways enough to breathe easier.

Her clothes were soaked, and her toes squished inside her boots. It was cold enough that her breath clouded the night air like a ghost. Sudden panic hit her. She hurried to check her pocket for the nut and found it in the same spot she'd put it. Horra sighed in relief.

Pidge darted after a squeaking creature, catching it and tossing it in the air with her ebony beak before swallowing it whole. The vine Horra had used in the castle still hung from the bird's neck.

"Where in the Wilden Lands did you drop me, Pidge?"

The pudge wudgie sent her a reflective golden stare. A rustle gained the bird's attention and it dashed off, on the hunt again, into a massive forest Horra didn't recognize. She'd never let Pidge out of the castle before. Would she fly off to ... who knew where?

Horra's pulse raced. "Don't run off and leave me here all alone." Her voice hitched and she coughed to keep a sob from coming forth. Horra swallowed her fear to figure out where they were.

What would Woodsly tell her to do? *Don't panic! Gather your wits and take stock.* And, *dry those boots out or you'll get the crud.* That thought sobered her.

She studied the sky as she removed her soaked boots, dumped them out, and tried to recall the basics she'd learned to start.

Rivers flowed north to south. From the castle, giants were to the west and ogres to the east. Horra could point it all out on a map, but she didn't have one with her. Even if she had, there was no way of telling what landmarks were here, if any.

Her goal, the Weald, was south of the castle, past Hobgoblin Pass, and centered amid the goblin lands. The best guess to her location was that Pidge had traveled west from the castle. That meant this stream could be one of three that flowed out of the Black Sea of the frozen lands in the far north. She'd camp out here for the evening and take off headed south toward the Weald in the morning.

Horra whistled for Pidge. She shivered and checked the sack. It was damp, but the clothes inside were not nearly as bad as what she currently wore. She pulled out a change of clothes and socks, which would help keep her warm. Once changed, she wrung the wet clothes out, smoothed them out over a boulder, and whistled for the pudge wudgie again.

"Pidge," Horra called out as she searched up and down the border of the forest, with no luck. After what seemed like hours and a raw, hoarse throat, Horra gave up, positive she'd seen her pet for the last time. At least she could take comfort in knowing the fairies wouldn't be butchering her beloved pet.

Thinking of the fairies reminded her of what she left behind. Her breath caught in her chest. What was happening with her father? What would happen to her kingdom now that the fairies and the hooded man had taken it over? Would their subjects be in danger?

The questions spun like blades of a fan in her gut until it burned like bile. She had no answers. The best she could do was take one step at a time. And right now, she needed to rest. It had been a long, confusing day and she was too exhausted to think anymore.

Shoulders slumped, Horra unbuttoned the side pocket for the tent and sleeping bag. Made from the rarest wyvern skin, the tent could stop an arrow and remain comfortable and waterproof even in below-zero temperatures. She'd used it during Woodsly's Wandering Wilderness classes.

It had always been so silly, camping out in the Conservatory to 'survive.' Looking back at this moment, she was almost grateful that, though the others paired up, Woodsly had made her do everything herself. Maybe if she tried, she could make it seem as though it was just another Wandering Wilderness test. Only this time, she wouldn't have to worry about her instructor pulling out his measuring stick and grading every little thing.

Though she hated magic, the sleeping bag became her favorite item since hers automatically inflated and deflated as she rolled it out or up. The others had been forced to blow theirs up. She'd gloat a bit that she didn't have to do so much work to cover the pang of having to do it alone. Her classmate Torren would always tease that he was going to reverse the sleeping bag's spell so she'd fail. He never had.

She almost missed the back-and-forth needling. She would've given anything, including letting him win an argument, to have him here right now badgering her on how taut her lines were. It was much worse being alone and wondering if her classmates, and her subjects, were safe.

Sticks cracked in the distance on Horra's left. She froze with the tent in her hands, ready to run. Pidge streaked through the thick pine limbs and stopped beside her.

She let out a loud puff of air. "You're worse than a hoarhound, running around like you're never fed and scaring poor trolls like me." She blew out a gust of air, loath to admit that it was reassuring to have at least one friend with her at the moment. Even if that one friend was a bird. "I guess you've always been caged up, huh, girl? Probably feels amazing being free in this big world." A huge world full of who knew what?

Pidge clucked in satisfaction, like she always did after being well-fed, and fluffed out her feathers. Horra grabbed the vine and tied it to a tree limb to keep her pet from straying again. She'd cut it off later.

She could hear Woodsly's detailed instructions in her mind, telling her how far the pegs should be hammered and how straight the top of the tent ought to be. She always had to reset the pegs because it was hard to create the tension needed on her own. The others never got any marks on that. She always had.

But Woodsly would never give her another mark on his parchment. Never again. Even if he regenerated, he'd become a different person. It was hard to see through the tears that welled in her eyes as she hammered and pulled to get the tent set up, just as if her instructor were there with her.

Horra finished setting up the tent between two stringy pine trees. A few branches placed on the top and sides would help hide it until she woke in the morning. Once inside, she unrolled the sleeping bag and embraced the small pleasure of watching it fill with air. Only it wasn't quite as satisfying as it once was.

She was tired and achy, almost like she was bruised from the tip of her red head to the bottoms of her black, clawed toes. One large, sorry, body-sized bruise.

And her heart, the most battered and beaten of all.

SUNLIGHT FILTERED through the spaces Horra hadn't placed limbs the night before. The shadows of the limbs were jagged, like claw marks against the scaly material of the tent. It didn't help her apprehension.

Her body protested moving, but she worked her way from sitting to standing inside the tent, stretching her bruised and aching limbs one by one. Though it had been quiet after she and Pidge settled last night, the events of the day haunted her sleep. With a flick of her wrist, she triggered the sleeping bag to deflate, rolled it up, and put it back in her sack. Inside the canvas pack, she touched a book and pulled it out.

Had she left a school book in the knapsack the last time she used it?

"Medicinal Curse book? This isn't my book. How did it get in here?" She opened the tent and stepped out. A couple of limbs fell to the side, and bright sunlight momentarily blinded her.

Pidge darted out of the tent past her, the vine dragging on the ground. She'd been too tired to remove it last night, and Pidge hadn't minded. Horra tossed the book and bag on the rocky ground. A paper stuck in the pages of the book fluttered in the breeze. Woodsly's crisp, neat handwriting covered the sheet.

Her throat tightened as she read it.

Princess Horra, if you find this, know you are in danger. Be on alert! I fear the Erlking has been reborn. Trust no one!!

I've been poisoned and must revert to a seed before the poison spreads too far and kills me fully. I implore you to take my seed to the Weald so I can regenerate. It must be done within a fortnight.

Trust me when I say if left unchallenged, the Erlking will become all-powerful. He'll send another plague, worse than the first one, upon the land. The Wilden Lands will become a wasteland ruled by an unimaginable evil.

Use this book to help you on your journey. My task as the last living druid has been to instruct the next grand warrior, namely you. I have done my best to make you ready for the challenge.

You are worthy, my Princess. Chin up. Use your head. And make your mother, and all your foremothers, proud.

Your humble instructor, Woodsly

Horra swiped her sleeve across her nose. The seed bulged in her pocket and she pulled it out. The now bright green leaf was completely unfurled. She recalled Woodsly's druid lessons.

Several generations ago, a druid priest predicted there would be a plague that would overtake the Wilden Lands such as had never been seen before. The harbinger was a threat to the druid line, which kept the magical balance in all the lands. Rumors through the years had been disproven and debunked until two generations ago.

That's when the Erlking unleashed the plague of withering warts, starting the war. Before Horra's grandmother slew the Erlking, he'd cast one last curse over the land, claiming another, greater Erlking would come, and it wouldn't be a plague he brought next time.

Woodsly claimed that only a druid would be able to stand in the way of the next Erlking should he come. But, many of the druids had died due to the plague breaching woodgoblin's barks, making them susceptible to illness and rot.

Trolls were affected as well, though their hide was several layers thicker and heartier. It was the elderly and the very young who died. Other creatures died by the dozens.

Horra's grandmother, Queen Petra, sent out a call for war. The War of the Warts lasted seven long years until the Erlking was killed by Petra's own hand. However, he'd cast that last curse over the land before his final breath. Horra never thought much of it before.

A tornado ripped through her gut now at the thought.

If the hooded man was the second coming of the Erlking and he wasn't bringing a plague, what was he doing? How did the fairies fit into his plan? What could it all mean?

Whatever it was, this was worse than just her castle and kingdom being affected. Woodsly was never one to be dramatic. She'd known something dire was afoot when he'd reverted to his seed form. Now she was positive. She stared at the seed, wishing he could give her more answers. But it was silent.

Just then, Pidge dodged for the seed and nabbed it from her hand.

CHAPTER 9

Horra fought her pet, feathers flying, to get ahold of the seed once more. After several attempts and rolling on the ground, she got the seed away from the bird. "Bad girl! You can't eat our only hope to save the Wilden Lands!"

Pidge's rebuke was shrill and loud.

"No seeds for you!" Horra pointed a claw at her pet's beak. Her stomach twisted in hunger. By now, the bird would've been fed and watered properly in the Conservatory. Her shoulders slumped. "Go on, find yourself something to eat. Just don't get lost."

The pudge wudgie gave her a side glance before trudging off into the woods in search of just that. Horra cleared the site, packing everything back into her knapsack. She searched the bushes at the edge of the forest for any sources of berries or edible mushrooms but found none.

Soon, pidge returned, clucking happily, and Horra dug out her compass. It pointed south, and they set out.

The stream meandered, starting and stopping in confusing ways. Several times she had to halt because she'd been preoccupied and not paying enough attention to where she was going. Too many thoughts crowded her mind to think clearly. Mudheadedness, Woodsly called it.

A glance at her trusty instrument showed she was headed south, the correct direction, but something wasn't right. She should've been in meadows by now, or at least close by them, not still in mountainous forests.

Frustration prickled as hot as her sweat and she shook her navigational guide. The needle spun around and around. What? It shouldn't do that, should it? It never had before.

She eyed the giant woody trees with great trunks. The arrow settled, pointing west instead of south like it indicated, toward a large, striped boulder. The sun, having risen in the same direction, told her that was wrong.

Why was it acting so strange? The only thing that could throw it off was—

Magnetized rocks! Vinegar!

What direction had she been going?

Pidge screeched and dodged into the tall limbs off to Horra's right, tracking some kind of animal, no doubt. She sighed and followed her pet.

Bushes with wide, fuzzy leaves up to her waist lined the ground leaving no path to walk. Black flowers in the center of the plants lifted their petals skyward as they opened, flooding the air with a sickening stench. Hundreds of pods hung from the stems, ripe for the picking.

She froze. *Witchbane.*

Its seeds were dried and ground to make prickly powder. The milky secretions from the stems were used in potions. Without being mixed with other plants, however, the secretions caused painful welts, even through thick troll hide.

Horra coughed and then gagged when the scent filled her open mouth. She stepped back carefully to avoid breaking any of the leaves or stems and retreated in the direction she'd come.

The ground beneath her feet shifted, and rumbles sounded in the distance. She glanced through the trees at the sunny sky. Not thunder.

The ground shook again. Horra hesitated. A distant noise, like a gurgling grumble, resounded. Gigantic birds, which made Pidge look like a hatchling, took flight and leaves rained down on Horra.

A sudden dawning of where she was hit her. She'd been near here once, years ago, with her mother. *Oh, please be wrong!* She turned to run in the opposite direction, away from the land of the giants. Her legs pumped hard, and the knapsack bounced against her back. Her tunic stuck to her hide in the heat.

Horra dodged from stringy pine tree to stringy pine tree, but the farther away she ran, the more open it became. She was a moving target.

"Birdy!" A rumbling voice burst out accompanied by heavy footfalls which quaked the ground.

Oh, no! Dread slammed into her stomach. The giant was after the pudge wudgie. In her instruction book, *Beasties: An Instruction Guide*, it stated that giants were playful but lethal because of their sheer size. It warned that care should be taken because giants were known for inadvertent strangulation deaths.

She peeked out from behind the pine. The giant was bent over searching for something. Having never seen a real giant in her life, Horra wasn't sure if it was a child or an adult. From this angle, she couldn't tell if it was a male or a female, either.

The giant clapped. "Birdy!" Its delighted squeal filled the air.

A child? But was that a good thing?

Horra closed her eyes and seized hold of whatever broken pine limbs were near her and put them over her legs for camouflage. The knapsack kept her from flattening herself completely against the tree, but that couldn't be helped. The distance between her tree and the next was too far to manage without being seen.

Heavy footfalls crunched closer and closer.

Where was Pidge?

A thump jounced her from behind. If only she weren't so small and slow. If only she could wink out of sight like the fairies! She ground her fangs together while biting her lip.

Sticks crackled, and the debris on the ground to her right moved. Warm breath washed past her right arm.

Horra sat ramrod stiff.

"Birdy?" The giant's hand darted to her left side. Pidge fluttered around Horra in a wide circle.

She shooed her pet, motioning silently with her hands.

"Dolly!"

The limbs she'd hidden under scratched as she dashed out of them, but she ignored the stings. Her knapsack thumped against her back as she ran, zigzagging through the trees to avoid the large boulders that stuck out of the ground.

Twigs snapped, and the ground rattled with each step the giant gained on her. Ahead of them, the forest thickened slightly, so she ran in that direction, hoping to lose the giant. She pushed her burning, sore legs and was about to enter the line of trees when the giant grabbed her.

The air was knocked out of Horra's lungs. In the distance, Pidge screeched. The hand holding Horra loosened, and she gulped in a grateful breath. She dug her claws into the massive hand holding her, but the giant didn't let go. Wind rushed across her face as she was lifted into the air. She pounded on the fingers clutching her to no avail.

"Dolly!" shrieked the giant child. Her voice made Horra's ears ring.

Up close, Horra could see flecks of blue in the brown eyes. Freckles spread across its orange cheeks. Ears, the size of Horra's torso, jutted out of a partially shaved head. Jewels and tattoo lines decorated the shaved part of the head, while a tuft of dark brown hair stuck out the top. Horra twisted away as it smashed its lips against her.

EW! Now she'd have to take another bath.

"Wait until Grendel sees!" The giant switched Horra from one hand to the other, and the knapsack fell to the ground.

"No!" Horra's protest was drowned out by the giant child's laughter. She managed to see which direction they were headed before she lost sight of her knapsack.

Horra tried to watch where they were going, or for any visual signs she could use to get back to the knapsack. However, it was impossible.

Swing up, pine needles smacked her head. Swing down, she hung halfway upside down. And then it started again. Up. Down. Up. Down. Up. Finally, the swinging motion ended.

Horra's head spun and her stomach reeled. Scratches on her face throbbed, and debris stuck in her hair.

Before them was a massive house. Another giant lounged in a chair, reading a book double the size of Horra's bed. A table next to the other giant held a glass of yellow liquid. Obviously, the child's home.

"Grendel! Look." The child thrust Horra out.

Horra bit back a nasty retort. These giants were big enough to squash her like a bug if they wanted, and she didn't intend to give them reason to smash her to a pulp.

Grendel didn't look up from reading an enormous-sized book. "That's nice, Galumph."

"It's my new dolly. Do you wanna play with me?"

Grendel glanced up from the book, and her thick-rimmed glasses slid down her nose. She pushed them back in place, making her eyes bulgy. "You didn't feed another critter cookies, did you?"

"Nuh-uh. I found it in the forest just like this." Galumph shoved her hand out again, and Horra's head snapped back painfully.

This new giant had the same orange skin and darkish hair, shaved on both sides with jewels like the child's. Freckles dotted her cheeks as well. She took Horra from the child, turning her this way and that.

Horra's stomach lurched and she choked on bile.

Grendel leaned in close enough that Horra smacked the lens of her glasses. Her claw barely grazed the glass, leaving no mark behind. "Galumph, I don't think this thing is safe. I've never seen anything so green and warty before. And its face is as red as its fur. I think you made it mad. You'd better put it back where you found it, or it might bite you or give you some kind of disease."

Hope filled Horra. Maybe Galumph would return her and she could get her knapsack and return on her journey of taking Woodsly to the Weald. She contorted her face and grunted, giving the giant her best fierce look.

Galumph shook her head. "I've seen these before, Grendel. Daddy says they're just silly old trolls. This one's not even big enough to bite me."

Unable to bend over and bite the hand, Horra snapped her jaws and clawed at the air.

Grendel *tsked*. "Okay, fine. Whatever. It still looks rabid to me. I'm not going to play with you. I want to finish reading this before tomorrow."

Rabid? Horra almost wished she was so the girl would let her go.

Happily, the child took Horra back. The child's sweaty hand with a pungent cheesy odor almost smothered Horra. She thrashed back and forth to get air.

Up Horra swung, and then back down. Over and over again as the child giant skipped.

More bile burned Horra's throat, but the child's hold was too tight to cough. Inadvertent strangulation, that's how she was going to die.

Galumph entered the massive stone house. Inside were furnishings as tall as the castle. She'd need a rope. And maybe a boost. Woven rugs covered the floors—bright and colorful with strange geometric designs. Enormous portraits of giants hung from the walls, like a massive Hall of Monstrosity. Only the monstrosity wasn't the beasts, but the orange giants instead.

She gulped at the smiling faces, their eyes seeming to follow her as the child skipped across the room. Did giants eat trolls? Her heart beat with doomed thumps in her chest.

Instead of a kitchen, down the hallway, they entered an expansive child's room. The girl plopped down on the floor next to a metal, miniature playset of a house. Miniature at least for giants. She tossed Horra onto a wooden toy bed in one of the bedrooms. "Dolly welcome home."

It was a nice change of pace, but it was definitely not her home. She'd always been small, but never quite so bug-sized small.

Horra rolled to her feet and backed away from the girl. The tiny room was too small to stand up in, so she bent over to get away, but the child had already lost interest in her.

"Now to find some playmates." She picked up a stuffed

dragon toy twice Horra's size and skipped from the room, slamming the door behind her.

Playmates? What kind of playmates did a giant child have? Horra swallowed hard, her throat tense with all kinds of horrible thoughts.

CHAPTER 10

Fast as she could, Horra poked her head out of the playset and studied the side going down. She was in an upstairs part of the toy house and below her the giant's room had a stone floor. Too far to jump without getting hurt. She took in the triangle-shaped room. There was only a wooden bed in it and a small cloth-like blanket. A dresser, lamp, and closet were painted on the metal walls like a mural. Round window frames held no glass, and the sides of the house were smooth metal.

Vinegar. Her shoulders slumped. Deflated, she flopped down to sit on the floor and contemplate. Between fear and the up-and-down trip to the house, Horra's stomach was all twisted in knots.

What would everyone think of her now? Her fierce and fearless mother? Or her father, who rarely paid her any attention? Had she failed them somehow, getting lost and then caught by a giant? She knew Woodsly would give her points off if this were a test.

But it wasn't a test. It was real life and she'd gotten herself in over her head right now. Literally. She closed her eyes and breathed deep to keep the well of hysteria from bursting forth. She needed to keep her wits. Make a plan. And stay calm above all else. Losing control wasn't going to help her.

She opened her eyes and took stock of the playhouse and the room.

A square of cloth covering the wooden-block toy bed would be no help. She considered the child's bedroom. Sunlight shone in from a partially opened window with a wooden table below it. Beside the table was a giant-sized bed. Mirroring the playhouse, the bed's blanket spilled over the side to the floor. If she could get over there, she might be able to climb the blankets, get across the table, and climb out the open window.

In the corner of the bedroom, she spied a mouse. Though normal-sized, it was but a teeny fizzbug in the enormous room. It stood on its haunches and glared at her. It twitched its pink nose, turned around, and left the room through a crack in the floorboard.

Creepy!

But how to get out of the dollhouse without breaking something? She wished she had her knapsack. She could've inflated the sleeping bag, thrown it down, and landed on it. Her nose itched from unshed tears, and she swallowed a mouthful of spit to keep from throwing up.

Warrior trolls didn't cry, and Horra hated to do so. Her eyes got all red and puffy and her nose stuffed up. She could cry later when she got out of here.

Loud, *thunking* footfalls reverberated through the room, followed by the giant child's laughter. The door opened, and she skipped in, holding the largest plumy catterwump Horra had ever seen. The child sang to the bright orange bug, which twisted and wriggled in her grip.

Pidge loved to eat the plumy catterwumps that the

hobgoblins collected from the pokeweed plants. A small group of catterwumps could decimate their small garden in the Conservatory in a few days—growing bigger and bigger as they ate. Because catterwumps were abundant everywhere, they were stored in a terrarium in the lab and fed to Oddar's exotic animals as treats.

But how'd one get this far north? And how'd it grow so big? It was almost the same size as Horra.

A circle on the top of the catterwump's head reminded her of a cyclops' eye. Its numerous horns moved around, each in a different direction. Horra caught the girl looking toward her, so she backed up to the bed, bumping into it. Her boots slipped on the blanket. There was nowhere to go when the child reached in and snagged her.

"Kissy." Horra was smushed against the slimy bug's cyclopean eye while the child made kissing noises. "Cattertrolls kissy."

Nasty-smelling goo spread across her mouth and nose. Horra choked and gagged.

The child giggled at her.

Horra thrashed back and forth, but the child was too strong. She swiped the snotty residue off on her sleeve. A bitter taste lingered on her lips.

"Galumph." Someone called from a distance. The child dropped Horra and ran out of the room.

Horra landed with an "oomph" back in the dollhouse. She wiped the catterwump's slime off on the blanket cloth and turned around.

She wasn't alone. The catterwump slunk, foot by foot, toward her.

Horra'd only known the bugs when they were small enough to hold in her claw. It hadn't been intimidating then. It was much scarier this size, with its eye, waving horns, and dozens of feet all headed at her. It emitted several low guttural noises.

"Easy there, buggie boy." Horra moved to the inside wall. When they were bug-sized she'd never noticed the hairs on each of its horns and the two mandibles which were currently snapping open and shut. It inched toward her, lifting its torso enough to come face-to-face with her. Saliva dripped from its jaws. Was it hungry? Horra edged closer to the open rim of the dollhouse. "Nice catterwump." Her voice wobbled and cracked.

It bounded at her. Horra jumped back and teetered, losing her grip on the slick wall of the playset. She tumbled over the side and landed on her hip—beside the pocket which held the seed. "Ow!"

Horra rolled over and dug the seed out of her pocket. It still had a slight glow to it and there were no cracks. "I always said you were a pain in my side, Woodsly!" It wiggled in her claw, and she shoved it back in her pants.

Back up on the dollhouse, the catterwump slithered inch by inch down the side seam, its cyclopean eye staring at her. Her heart pounded, causing the bruise on her backside to beat like a drum.

Now that Horra was on ground level, she gathered a better look at her options. The mouse's crack in the floorboard was too small for her. The table legs and wall were too smooth to climb. The space beneath the door was too narrow for her to crawl through. She'd been right about the blanket being her best chance. She ran over to it.

She grasped hold of the silky fabric to climb up, but it slipped. Her foot tangled in something weblike. Inside the wispy strings was a hairy, eight-legged creature: a torentula. Intimidating enough at its regular size, this spider, like the catterwump, was larger than normal.

What in twisted terrariums was going on?

Horra yanked her booted foot, but she only ended up getting more tangled. Her legs were now encased in the sticky threads. With every move, she became more entwined. Panting from the effort, Horra stopped moving. She had only made it halfway up the bed, clinging to the slick bedding and stuck to the web, and she was already spent.

The torentula glided across the web toward her. No one must ever have cleaned underneath the bed because it was a maze of dusty webs, bug carcasses, and egg sacs. The threaded network spanned the whole underside of the bed from the floor to the frame.

Ogre's eye! What madness had she gotten stuck in?

Horra leaned away, and her right arm became stuck. "Ugh."

The catterwump made a gurgling moan, stopping the motion of the spider toward her.

With an eye on the torentula, Horra reached out her left hand and snipped at the fibers holding her hostage with her sharp clawnails.

More groans resonated from the catterwump. Horra didn't care if it was trying to communicate with her. She wanted to get as far away from it, this torentula, and the giant child as she could.

The torentula darted out from under the bed, straight at the catterwump, each hair on its spindly legs alert.

Horra snipped and yanked until she was loose. Down she slipped out of the web, plunging to the floor, but she managed to catch hold of the blanket. Claw over claw she climbed until she reached the edge of the mattress.

Below her, the two immense bugs faced off. The catterwump growled. The torentula, legs bent at attention, circled it.

Footsteps sounded just outside the door. The spider streaked back underneath the bed. Horra made one last lunge and hauled herself over the edge of the bed and onto the top.

The child skipped into the center of the room and stopped. The catterwump crept leg over leg toward the bed but was much slower than the spider. The child picked it up and then glanced toward the dollhouse.

"Dolly? Where are you?"

Horra shuffled under the blanket to hide, making sure to get a clear view in case she needed to move fast.

"Dolly?" she cried out louder.

"Naptime, Galumph." A female giant stepped into the room. She was much bigger than the child. Same orange, freckled skin, and shaved, bejeweled scalp. She wore a grand dress with enough fabric to curtain the whole castle.

Horra backed up further inside the blanket, far enough so she could only just see the giants.

"But, my new dolly," whimpered the child.

The mother sighed. "Where did you leave it last?"

"In the dollyhouse."

The mother took the child's hand, and they examined the toy house and the enormous bookshelves. They came back around to the bed, and the mother flipped the blanket up onto the bed.

Horra practically swam through the sheet to get away before the blanket landed back down. She shimmied to the opposite side, near the top under a pillow.

"We'll find it after your nap." The mother picked Galumph up, and, despite the girl's protests, sat the child down on the bed, causing it to bounce.

Horra slid to the opposite side of the pillow and along the bedframe. She bounced around as the mother tucked the child in.

"Nighty-night."

"Dolly," Galumph yawned.

"I promise we'll find it or get a new one after your nap, little one." The mother kissed the child on her forehead. "Sweet dreams." She shut the door quietly behind her.

Horra's heart twisted for a painful moment. She remembered her mother doing the same thing. And for a moment, she envied the child. That moment ended quickly when she realized Galumph had carried the catterwump to bed with her.

It poked its head over the child's shoulder and inched toward her.

CHAPTER II

Horra moved along the headboard toward the table. It was made of stringy pine, a ridged and pocked wood. She hooked her claw into one ridge and hefted herself up to grab ahold higher. She was close enough to escape and leave all this madness behind if she could climb over to the table.

Galumph shifted, causing the bed to move. One of Horra's claws slipped, but she dug into the wood with the other claw and her hiking boots. Again, the child shifted, flinging her arm, and bumping the headboard. Horra held tight, but her hold was tenuous and she was sweating.

Below her, the catterwump was moving, foot by foot, up the pillow, its cyclopean eye staring at her. A snail-like tongue slipped through its snapping mandibles as if tasting the air.

Horra's stomach dropped to her boots.

Galumph's breaths grew deeper until they ended in a snore. The child's countenance was peaceful in sleep.

Finally, she could make some real progress and get away from her pursuer.

The catterwump reached the headboard. Though Horra would have preferred to fall to the soft bed below, she shuffled sideways across the uneven wood. She hurried, but the ridges were hard to maneuver.

The bug's sticky tongue flicked out again. It had crossed half the headboard and was gaining ground. Horra glanced down, but the child's head was right below her. She couldn't jump down or she'd wake the child. Could she be fast enough to beat the catterwump to the table?

Her claws became sweatier, making it even harder to hold on. Galumph jerked in her sleep, and the headboard shook. One of the catterwump's horns tickled Horra's elbow, and she let go of the headboard, dropping to the bed below.

Horra landed with a poof on the pillow just above Galumph's head. The child's brown hair fluttered.

Horra's boots were almost touching the child's nose. She held her breath for a moment until she was sure the child was still asleep.

Galumph moved her arm again, and Horra slipped across and down the pillow, sliding between the bed and table. If she sweat anymore, she'd be soaked.

From this vantage, Horra spied the torentula climbing up the bed. Leg by spindly leg, the spider prowled up the side, from the same spot where she had gotten stuck in the web. It stopped, body alert with its front two feet waving in the air until it spotted the catterwump.

She needed to get out of here or one of those creatures would have her for dinner. Horra surveyed the side of the table. The wood wasn't stringy pine, but there were a couple of gouges she could use to climb. She dug one boot in and reached for the next indentation. Behind her, the catterwump let out a groan. The table edge was just above her head, and, though she stretched on her tippy claws, she couldn't quite reach it.

She leaned against the table to rest her arms. The torentula was halfway across the bed and the catterwump crawled across the child's hair toward Horra.

"Here goes nothing." Horra bent her knees, and, with her remaining strength, stretched. She wasn't tall enough. She dug her claws back into the wooden notches.

The catterwump growled with the torentula right on its tail. The child was still asleep, her eyelids moving back and forth in a dream.

Horra flexed her knees and jumped harder this time. Her claws touched the edge but failed to grasp the wood. She slid down the side of the table and back onto the mattress.

Vinegar and beans! Frustrated, Horra kicked the side of the table and flopped onto the mattress with her back against the table. A hunk of something fell off the table and landed on her head. More chunks rained down on her, so she put her arms up to protect her head. Crumbs covered her hair and clothes. A sweet scent wafted around her. She grabbed a crumb and tasted it. It resembled a delicious cookie. Her tongue tingled, but her stomach overruled her mouth.

Horra devoured several tasty hand-sized chunks and burped from eating so fast. Her father would've frowned at her. That stopped her cold, and her eyes stung again. Prickles crossed her hide. She had to get back to save her father and her kingdom. She closed her eyes to hold the emotions back. Her nose ran, and she sniffed.

Her head swirled, spinning dizzily, and then smacked against something. She opened her eyes. Her view had changed. She was right next to the giant child. And instead of looking across at the catterwump, she was looking down at it.

Startled, the catterwump curved its long body around and ran straight into the torentula.

Horra twisted back to the table. She didn't have to jump to get on the ledge now, she could simply climb onto it.

She examined her body. She'd grown. Even her legs were longer. Her clothes were tighter, too.

Galumph moaned in her sleep. The catterwump and torentula clashed. Back and forth they attacked each other. Their motion moved them closer to her. Horra couldn't believe they weren't waking the sleeping giant. That she, as big as she currently was, wasn't waking her.

She wasn't sure what had made her grow, though her mind whispered, *'magic.'* She didn't complain. It was saving her hide at this moment, and that's all that mattered. She needed to get out of here and now.

Without looking back, Horra climbed onto the table. Cookie crumbles littered the top along with a bag of chalky candy, which spilled across the surface. She grabbed the bag of candy and shoved in chunks of the cookie to eat later—after she'd escaped. The child wouldn't miss them, and Horra was starving.

A small web full of torentula eggs was clustered on the backside of the table. She snipped it loose with her claws and tucked them into an empty bag, sealing it tight, for Pidge.

A breeze from the open window caressed her face. Horra carefully walked across the table, praying it wouldn't collapse under her new weight. At the window, she stuck the bags into her empty pocket. Her other pocket no longer bulged.

"Oh, no!" she whispered. "I've lost the seed." She glanced back at the child asleep on the bed and across at the warring bugs. She couldn't go back in there now. But she had to have the seed.

CHAPTER 12

In a panic, she stuck her claw inside her pocket and searched for the seed. It was there, in a corner at the bottom. Her pocket hadn't bulged because the seed was smaller.

Relief tingled across her hide and she laughed at herself. Of course it was harder to find, she was bigger than ever before.

Galumph's soft snores joined the catterwump's deep rumbles. They clashed, and the catterwump with its girth easily overtook the torentula.

Horra turned from the grisly sight, lifted the window higher, and jumped.

The ground below was farther down than Horra realized, even though she'd grown bigger. She landed face-down in the grass.

A shape fluttered above her as she stood and brushed off dirt and debris.

A squeal pierced her ears, and she smiled. "Pidge! Hey, girl!"

Black as a shadow, the pudge wudgie settled next to her on

the ground, the vine still stuck to her neck. Horra, having grown, was now twice the size of the bird. She stroked the bird's inky feathers. "Look how big I am, Pidge. Oh, girl, you would've gone crazy over that giant catterwump!"

However, there was no way she would go back in to get it for her pet.

The pudge wudgie tipped her head back and forth at her. The seed jiggled in her pocket reminding her she needed to get to the Weald.

Pidge darted into the air.

"Hey, wait for me!" Horra hoped the bird was going in the right direction because she needed to find her knapsack.

Peeking around the stone house, there was only Grendel sitting in the same lounge chair, her nose still stuck in a book. She took a sip from a glass. Loud music drifted across the wind. The hair on the back of Horra's neck rose.

A guttural snarl erupted from Grendel. The music became intense, and she bent over in obvious pain.

Horra stepped back and scanned the area. Where were they? The Erlking and the fairies had to be close by.

Tufts of fur spread across Grendel's hands. She snarled, her teeth lengthening. Horra's heart raced in her chest. Was it the music? She recalled the deaf servant being the only one unaffected by it. She needed to get out of here.

Palms blocking her ears, Horra dashed across the yard in the direction she remembered Galumph bringing her. She was too nervous to fully delight in how fast her longer legs were. And now that she was taller, she spied a worn path that must've been used by the child. Pidge circled above the trail.

Horra ran with her head down, closely following the pathway.

Eventually, she slowed and dropped her claws from her ears. There was no music here, only birds chirping and wind rustling through the trees. She smelled the witchbane before the plants came into view as she broke through the trees. She'd have to travel through it to get back to her knapsack.

She kept to the sparser side, careful she didn't break any of the limbs or leaves. Thankfully, she made it out.

Pidge dropped down and squealed. A few feet ahead, Horra caught sight of the knapsack. It lay crumpled on the ground where it had fallen.

Yes! Finally, something's going right. She picked it up and hooked it on to her elbow. It was now too small to get fully across her back. It was much easier to carry. She took only a moment to study her body. Her pants now rested at her knees instead of brushing the ground. Her tunic was tight and came up past her elbows instead of down to her wrists. She sucked in a breath and realized her fangs weren't sharp and pointed but blunt and a claw-length wide.

"Strange things happen in giant's houses, Pidge. Very weird, indeed." She'd have to make it a point to study them, maybe ask Woo—a bird chittered in the trees near her, breaking her ponderings and reminding her she was on a mission. Her gut only pinched for a moment before thoughts of losing her instructor settled too far in, and tears couldn't be helped. "Time to get out of here, Pidge. We have important things to do."

And almost a day of wandering around lost to make up for.

THE SUN RESTED low by the time they found the stream again. The beaches and rocky areas which ran along the stringy pine trees all looked alike, so Horra couldn't tell if they were close to where they'd camped the night before. She was thirsty and hungry, so she found a clear area and stopped. She grabbed the bag, sat down, and cupped her claws to drink from the clear, running stream. It was cold and refreshing.

She leaned against a large boulder scattered along the rocky beach and opened the bag she'd stuffed at the giant's house. Inside the cookie was mushed into a big ball of mess. Luckily, the candy had a hard coating and remained untainted from the cookie. She tossed a couple of cookie chunks to Pidge and decided to eat the candy instead. It was sweet, but it had a twangy aftertaste.

Pidge fluffed her feathers once, twice, and then grew, first past Horra's head, and then taller. Oh, no! What was happening?

Horra's stomach gurgled, and she doubled over. When the rumbling passed, she sat up. Pidge was much now taller than she was. She glanced down at herself. Stubby legs with her pants' cuffs longer than she was tall. Her shirt back down to her wrists.

She was short again.

She groaned. Realization gripped her and she remembered the giant sister talking about the girl feeding cookies to the bugs. That's what it was! The cookies made you grow. The candy made you shrink.

Whatever this was, it was a complicated concoction, a mixture of magic and potion, something a troll couldn't do without another magical creature's help. It must be the same for giants since they had no magic to speak of. Giants relied on size, not potions or conjury. At least that's what she understood about them.

If not giants, who could have made these goodies, then? Why would the giants, especially a child like Grendel, have something this dangerous that shrunk or grew something larger?

Horra frowned. She detested magic, but she would travel

easier being bigger. And Pidge was harder to handle this much bigger than Horra—three large pudge wudgie gulps and Horra would be dinner for her ravenous pet. There was no choice. She put the candy aside and ate a hunk of the cookie. In seconds she became the same size as Pidge.

The only problem was her now-tight clothes. She pulled at the sleeves and waist, stretching them enough to have some relief.

A wave of heated exhaustion hit her. "Whew! That stuff's potent." Horra secured the bag and put it back in her pocket. She checked her other pocket to be sure she still had the seed.

She took it out and hugged it to her chest, hoping her escape would've made her instructor proud. The stem crumbled in her grasp, and she held it out to look at. It was still a nice brown color. Healthy-looking. She needed to get a move on and get to the Weald, but her body was weighted down like the boulder she sat against.

Pidge stomped her claws on the ground, her eyes fixed on a point in the tree line beside the rocky beach. The bird took flight, no doubt on the hunt again.

Horra didn't have the energy to set up a campsite, so she studied the area to figure out where she was and where she needed to go instead. Her eyes drooped. They were like lead— hard to lift.

She yawned. An orange glow of the setting sun radiated to her left. If she remembered correctly, this stream would've been to the west of Nomans Mountain and her castle, so the sunset was in the direction of her home.

Her jaw cracked with the strain of the next yawn. Her sight turned blurry.

Pidge's squeal of triumph from somewhere inside the trees blended into the outdoors noises. The stream's rippling hum lulled Horra. She relished the feel of the boulder she laid her head against, still warm from the day. She'd just close her eyes for a moment.

Her arms were numb when she roused. One side was warm from Pidge, who slept with her beak tucked beneath a wing beside Horra. The other side was cool from the night air. Fog blanketed the area, consuming the moonlight. She blinked her eyes to clear away the sleepy residue.

Surprise shot through her. *Hot vinegar!* How long had she slept?

She sat up and shook her arms to regain feeling. Pidge's body rose and fell as the bird slept. Horra's jacket rustled as she put it on, stretching it to fit over her shoulders. A seam ripped. The noise broke the thick silence. Was the fog muffling the sounds? Horra recalled the noises from last night when she lay safe beneath the cover of the tent. There'd been plenty of calls and rattling of nocturnal creatures scurrying and calling out.

Though Horra couldn't quite put her finger on it, something didn't feel right.

Horra grabbed the knapsack and hooked it around one arm. Her boots pinched, but not enough to take them off. She nudged the bird to wake her. The whites of Pidge's eyes contrasted against the hazy darkness. "Come on girl."

The wudgie stood slowly, looking around. The bird let out a low squeak and stood to stretch its wings.

"Shhh," Horra admonished. The air, already heavy with precipitation, thickened.

Horra walked close to the edge of the stream, trying to be quiet. She rubbed at her arms to still the goosebumps racing across her hide. She kept a sharp eye on the open beach and the tree line, devising a plan in case she needed to run.

Muted notes of music filtered through the haze. She stood still, eyes the only thing moving on her body. It was the same music that played at the giant's house when Grendel started to morph into something strange.

Shooting a glance in every direction, nothing moved or was out of place. The music kept playing, getting louder by the second. She hastened toward the tree line with Pidge following close above her.

A flash of light exploded behind them up the shore, reflecting off of the water.

Horra bit back a scream and bolted into the trees.

CHAPTER 13

Dense fog swirled around Horra's legs as she ran, keeping close to the tree line. Pidge was faster, but darted in and out of the trees in a meandering path, hunting as she went.

The piskie lights disappeared as they ran, but voices followed them as they raced away.

She dashed to hide behind the biggest tree she could find. Bent over, breathing hard, she tried not to make much noise. Not far away, Pidge's feathers glimmered as the bird flew and then darted after some unknowing prey. Seconds turned into minutes, and finally, Horra ventured out.

Pidge landed next to her, squealing.

"Quiet!" Horra scratched her neck. It looked safe enough, though safe didn't seem to apply anymore. She wished she'd gotten a better look at them. Had it been the hooded man? No, whoever it was had a wider built, stocky not gaunt. It hadn't sounded like the fairies. The voices were too gruff.

It could have been dwarfs who mined in the lower Iron Mountains. But why would dwarfs—unruly, smelly creatures who hoarded kobald metal to the exclusion of everything else and the detriment of any who stumbled upon their mines—have piskies?

They wouldn't. She stood and continued, picking her way through the forest in the quietest manner she could manage.

Daylight was bright overhead when she reached the end of the forests, arriving at the edge of the Iron Mountains. Trouble was, they went on for miles and she didn't know if it was the dwarfen lands or Oddar's mountains.

She came upon an unpassable drop-off. She'd have to scale down the mountains, heading west. She checked her compass just to be sure and shifted the backpack. With a whistle to Pidge, she trudged on.

The mountains went on endlessly. She'd never realized how many mountains and how hard it was to traverse before. If only she were a bird. Or she could travel by fairy path.

"*Pfth.* Trolls don't take shortcuts." She stepped around another large pine tree. They were all alike, nothing stood out as a visual landmark. She did have something that might make the trek easier, though. But, what would her foremothers say?

"Hard work is the bounty of a kingdom," she muttered. Surely if it were something that saved her and in doing so saved her kingdom and the whole Wilden Lands, it would be acceptable when necessary. They'd used magic to create the cure for withering warts, after all.

Horra flipped the bag over and sat down on a fallen log. Birds chirped around her and light mottled the shaded, rocky ground.

There were accepted levels of magic in Oddar. Magic was justified when it was helpful, a tool. Not when it was used exclusively for comfort as the fairies did.

She shook her head. The fairies would've probably found the Weald by now. They could've used their fairy paths to get out of the giant lands and traveled over the forested treetops in record time. It might be cheating, but it wasn't unsubstantial. Hard work was great when it got you closer to a goal. And so far, none of Horra's hard work had gained her a thing except to get lost.

The mountains could go on forever. She only had so much time, less than a fortnight now, to get to the Weald. She took the seed out and rubbed it. Having it grounded her, even if Woodsly was no longer here. She put it back in her pocket.

She continued, always down, down, down the steep rocky mountain. Pidge fluttered around, darting this way and that as she hunted. Horra reached a ridge and crept to the edge to look over. Pidge landed beside her, glancing down the side.

The sky was blue with few wispy white clouds. Sunlight was waning. Tips of trees and more rock greeted her, but below there was a flat area. There had to be villages nearby. She tried to figure out the least treacherous path, deciding to head right.

Halfway down the path, in a deep, shadowed nook, it became slick with snow. The only way down was to climb. Unlike the giant's bed, there were few claw and footholds. Chilled, Horra carefully picked her way down, slipping and sliding. She was almost to the bottom when her hand lost its hold. Without anything to grab hold of, she had no way of stopping.

Rocks rained down on her as she fell, bouncing on boulders. Young saplings whipped at her as she slid by. And then there was nothing beneath her at all.

CHAPTER 14

Horra lay, panting close to another ledge. She'd slid most of the way, and tumbled the rest. Her heart beat hard and her nose stung from heaving in breaths of cold air. She was two steps away from the edge of a steeper drop-off.

Her mouth was dry and her body ached from bumping down the mountain. Luckily, she still had the backpack, which had kept her backside safe after the dizzying drop landed her on a hard stone. She dug a handful of snow and chomped on it to soothe her thirst and tried to ignore the goosebumps.

Pidge screeched and landed beside her. The bird gave her an inquiring golden look.

"I'm fine. Mostly." Horra checked her pocket. The seed was still there, though damp.

The sun beat down from low in the sky. A brisk breeze rustled across the sparkling, snow-covered rock, buffeting her and whipping loose snow at her face. Fear sang through her blood, turning it to icicles. She choked out a scream and scootched carefully back away from the edge, resting on the top of the jutting rock.

They were closer than the giant lands, but it wasn't enough progress. She needed to gain more ground. Her eyes pinched closed. Only one way to do that.

Horra squeezed off a crumbly chunk of cookie and fed it to Pidge. She then ate a larger piece and waited for it to change her.

It wasn't as energy-sapping this time. She got to her knees and stood, gaining her bearings and finding an animal trail—a much safer distance from the ledge. Carefully, she trudged on, arms crossed over her chest and her eyebrows mashed together in concentration. By the end of the day, they'd made it off of the mountain. A glance back up at the lofty peak made Nomans, her home mountain, seem more like a hill.

Across the pasture, candlelight from windows in a village cast a golden glow. Closer up, Horra realized she and Pidge were taller than the doorways.

Bigger, smaller, smaller, bigger. All of the size changes were making her crazy.

Horra tossed a full-sized piece of candy to the bird and took a broken shard for herself. If Pidge was smaller than she, it would be easier not to lose her to someone who would harvest her parts.

She doubled over with stomach cramps as she shrank. She would never get used to changing. Pidge fluttered around on the ground, smaller than ever. Horra's clothes were a mess, so she dug in the knapsack for a fresh change. Now that she had shrunk again, she could wear them, and she hoped they wouldn't be quite as tight.

She donned her only other pair of pants, put a new shirt on, and topped it with her jacket. Her hair was sticking out in different directions, so she tore a small strip off of her first tunic and tied it back in a ponytail. It was still an unruly amount of curly hair even tied back.

She'd rarely been to other villages and never alone. If ever Woodsly would've been handy, it would've been now. He loved to drone on and on with facts about the different areas and creatures.

But he wasn't there. Horra checked for the seed which was still in her dirty pants. She transferred it to her new pair and picked up the pudge wudgie to scratch her neck. "Okay, Pidge. Stay hidden in my jacket or I'll have to put you in the knapsack." She flicked the hood up over her head with Pidge safely tucked inside. Her hair shifted as the bird quickly nested in her long hair. She pushed and shoved the excess until the hood was bursting with the red tresses. She growled. It was impossible to get everything inside the small hood. Horra grabbed at the strings and tugged them tight. Only her face showed now.

She walked along the dirt road leading into the village, moving to the side as a buggy rolled past. Bigger than a hamlet, a sign outside of the unfamiliar village simply said "Wester."

Streetlamps glimmered yellow upon the red brick road. Parchment announcements lined the wooden gates into the village. A bright white one among all of the worn advertisements and edicts caught her eye.

Her claws dug into her palms and she pinched her eyes shut. When she opened them, her own face stared back at her from the white sheet nailed to the wooden gate.

What in the name of banshee's bunions?

The sheet proclaimed that Princess Horra Fyd was the Wilden Land's number one criminal.

Wanted for assault of her father, King Divitri, for attacking over a dozen royal guests, including fairy princesses Misty and

Glory Toppenbottom, and for theft of endangered animals from the castle.

The reward was set at five hundred gold bars—a life's wages for most of the lands. She clutched her chest as surprise and shock rocked her.

Horra tore the sheet off and crumpled it. How had they gotten a picture of her? There was no official portrait until her coronation.

Her blood pulsed hot through her body. The only explanation was magic. Stupid, intrusive magic.

The ground beneath her rumbled with the approach of another carriage. Horra turned away, praying she wouldn't be noticed. How many of these parchments were hung across the Wilden Lands? It was rare for a lone troll female to be out of Oddar. It was rarer still to be a troll without green hair. Her royal red hair would be recognized.

Horra was glad she had the vapid vestra jacket and it was cool enough not to catch anyone's attention with her long hood pulled tight over her head. The fabric itself would help hide her appearance by mimicking her surroundings. Pidge was a warm ball against her neck.

She walked with her head down and her hands tucked inside the sleeves. She was taller, not quite as tall as her classmates, but tall enough not to seem like a babe walking around unescorted.

A lock of her red hair fell out of her hood, and she brushed it back quick, scratching her face. Enticing scents filled the air outside of a pub. A sign hanging over the door stated it was the Boar's Head Pub. Horra's stomach grumbled and Pidge chirped in her ear.

She grabbed to catch the pudge wudgie, but Pidge had already taken off. The bird was no bigger than a regular bird, but she was still unusual. Her pet could end up in a pie or a stew. Or worse. She couldn't let that happen.

Horra ran after her.

Pidge flew inside the pub just as someone walked out. Horra twisted away from them. She couldn't go in there. What if someone recognized her?

But she needed to get Pidge.

Vinegar!

She stood outside of the pub, hesitant. The door opened again, and a group of dwarfs came out, loud and laughing. Even with her back turned from them, they reeked of unwashed bodies. She drew closer to the next building, trying her best to blend into the stone exterior.

After several minutes of waiting, someone wearing a long, black cape came out. The person was tall and had to bend to step through the doorway. She flattened herself against the building until they walked away.

As she turned back, she spied Pidge nibbling at a piece of food on the ground. This was her chance. With a quick claw, she grabbed her pet and tucked her back into the hood. "You scared me. Don't do that again, girl!"

The door to the Pub opened again, and out staggered a drunken elf. He was silver and tall with white hair. His ears drooped down more than they pointed up. He had to be at least two hundred years old. His faded gray eyes locked on Horra before she could turn away.

He opened the Pub door and yelled back inside. "I found her. The troll princess! Sound the alarm!"

CHAPTER 15

Horra ran, trying not to trip on the cobblestones, staying close to the edge of the street to not get run over by a carriage or horse. The street twisted to the left and then to the right, then led straight into a wall. She stopped to listen, but there was only the thrumming of her heart pounding loud in her ears. Blessedly, there were no shouts or slapping feet against the bricks.

She sat down and caught her breath. Pidge, who had been clinging to her collar as she ran, popped her inky head out of Horra's hair. "Naughty bird! That was too close."

Voices and footsteps sounded from her left, so she pulled the hood down over her face and tucked her claws into her sleeves. A couple of minutes passed by, and the voices disappeared.

She needed to find a way to disguise herself. She stood up and walked back down the alley and tried to remember which direction she'd run from, but everything was identical. All of the cottages were the same shape, painted either a dull white or tan, and all had brown roofs.

It probably didn't matter which one she chose, she just needed to find a way out of this hamlet. Pidge fluffed her feathers and nested back behind her neck.

It would have been so much easier to fly off, over the village to safety. But she couldn't, so she kept ambling along the bricked streets, staying silent and in the shadows as much as possible.

Five turns later, Horra was still as lost as she was before, just in a different dark alley. How could one small hamlet be this hard to get out of? She tucked the coat closer around her and walked with her head down.

After a few steps, Horra stumbled into someone. A tall, hulking someone. She stepped back and mumbled an apology, but was grabbed by her arms and lifted upwards.

"What have we here? A girl out in the middle of the night with nobody around to protect her?"

Her chest was as tight as the grip on her arms. It was the tall, caped figure from the pub. He was a bocan!

The goblin had a shaved head, with one half tattooed black and the other painted white. Tusks protruded from his earlobes, and viper fangs were knotted to a cord around his neck. Horra shivered. She'd almost rather be in the child giant's hands right now.

Best to act ignorant and maybe he'd think she was a mere child out wandering around. "Pardon me, sir. I meant no harm. Please forgive the trespass."

He held her tighter and squinted his eyes at her.

She bit back a squeal at the painful grip, instead inhaling his disgusting alcohol-laden breath.

"You're a troll. What's a troll doing here?"

It didn't seem as if he recognized her. Horra remembered her father talking about bocan's stupid but violent nature. Goblin mercenaries without brains or mercy.

Money and reward were their motivation. "Just bartering, sir."

A twinkle lit his eyes, and he held her out farther. "What're you bartering for?"

"My mistress is in dire straits. Put me down and I'll show you." Pidge fluffed out her feathers, tickling Horra's neck.

"Don't try anything unwise." His smile was dimmed by jagged, blackened teeth. He sat her down and flipped a weapon from his pocket.

Even in her larger state, he was easily thrice her size, and she noted the dozens of lines cut into his upper arms which bulged out from the cape. Scars of conquest, no doubt. She eyed his curved knife crusted with dirt. And dried blood.

Horra took a step back and opened her knapsack. She reached inside and fumbled until she found the compass. It wasn't worth much. The next thing she found was the book.

"Well?" He sliced the blade he held down the side of her head and a few pieces of her red hair fell to the ground.

Horra stilled. In her whole life, no one had ever cut her hair. Not even her mother had so much as trimmed it. It wasn't done. She gripped the jeweled dagger and fury made her eyesight dim for just a hesitant moment.

"I'm getting impatient." Spit flew from his lips.

She glanced back at the knife. Its tip stuck in the dirt at her boots. Quick as she could, she pulled the dagger from her sack and held it out. "Nobody touches my hair," she spoke quietly, trying to rein in her anger.

The menace wasn't lost on the bocan. He moved back, not a full step, but far enough to give Horra breathing space.

The only physical sport Horra had been allowed was archery. But the dagger was razor sharp, the blade nearly unbreakable. Made from kobald, mined from the dwarf-owned mountains she'd just left, and onyx, the blade was impossible to not recognize as priceless. It alone would carry weight she couldn't muster.

He eyed the dagger, a gleam in his eyes. "You talk a good game for such a small threat. You might stick me once with that, but you won't get a second chance."

She knew what he implied. She could hurt him, but not fatally. And she wouldn't get an upper hand on him. "Not a threat. It's a promise." His eyes were dark and Pidge was getting restless against the tight muscles of her neck.

"Hmm. It would be a good fight to win." He leaned back and crossed his arms in front of his chest. Not enough to end the threatening posture, but relaxed enough to ease the strain in her lungs. "I want the dagger," he growled.

Horra narrowed her eyes at him. The weapon, with its encrusted jewels, dug into her palm as she clenched it, still holding it at a dangerous angle.

"An even trade. Safe passage, Princess, for the pretty dagger." He smirked. "Or I could turn you in. You decide."

She blinked then gulped. He'd seen the posters. Or figured it out from her red hair. Either way, she was sunk. Her mind whirled, trying to come up with a better solution, but she came up blank.

"I'm headed to Hobgoblin Pass. I'll go no farther. My word you'll be safe until we reach my stop." His eyes glittered. He knew he had her.

And it rankled. He knew who she was and that he could get a life's wages if he turned her in. But the dagger was priceless. He could bargain for more than money with it. But could she trust him? Magic folk could use spells and make sure whoever they did business with didn't go back on their word. But she didn't have any magic to bind the bocan to his word.

The upside was that the bocan couldn't bind her to anything, especially anything against her will. However, without an oath she could hold him to, he had the upper hand. Unless they did a blood oath. The magic of the dagger could hold them both to their words.

Horra grinned. At least the long, boring Goblin Courts were paying off. Woodsly would be so proud of her.

"I demand a blood oath or no deal. Safe passage, as in you won't touch me or what's mine, and I'll get to your destination free and alive, not shackled and starved. And you tell nobody who I am or that I'm traveling with you. If you do, you'll surrender your life."

His smug smile dropped to a hard line. Possibly, she surprised him with her intelligence. Bocans were notorious for their crooked deals. She dropped her arm some—enough to ease the tension but not enough to end her unspoken bluff. Oh, she'd stab him if she had to, but his bargain changed that. Hobgoblin Pass was nearer to the Weald than she'd been since she left the castle.

They stared at each other, his right eye twitching, her gaze unblinking.

CHAPTER 16

"Fine." He held out his hand.

She slit his palm enough to draw blood and did the same with hers. They both clutched the dagger. Magic like a gust of wind battered against them, sealing the bargain.

He dug a cloak out of a bag strapped to his back. "Put this on and don't talk."

Horra took the cloak from him in exchange for the dagger. She held on to the weapon for a second longer than expected, but he only grunted at her. She didn't want to let her mother's prized blade go. She wouldn't if she had any choice. She didn't, so she let it go with a silent apology to her mother for being stupid enough to get caught.

The cloak was heavy and black, much longer than she was tall, even though she'd grown since eating the cookie. It had sleeves that covered her arms past her long claws. She tied it under her chin and again in the center, just above her knees. The hood was much too large, however, so she left it dangling down her backside. Besides, she had her own head covering. She'd be fine.

"Follow me." He strode off without waiting for her to comply.

Horra tripped on the fabric dragging at her feet. The bocan kept walking without looking back. She fisted the material and hurried after him.

He led Horra to a wagon with low side rails hitched to two restless Stempner steeds. Her father owned a Stempner—a specialized, large breed of horse from the lost Endwylde lands. She was never allowed to ride them because, besides being imposing at twenty hands tall, they were wild and easily spooked. Their hooves were excessively large as well and could break a troll's back easier than snapping a stick.

Thinking of her father made her heart contract in her chest, and she turned away so the bocan wouldn't see the tears in her eyes.

The empty wagon was made of thick wood and had solid, ridged-metal wheels. Though sturdy looking, the shallow bed was suspicious. "How are you planning on hiding me in this contraption?" Horra asked while swiping at her nose. "And what's your name?"

"Keep that cape pulled tight around you. Don't talk. Don't draw attention to yourself. That's how. And the name's Balk." He hefted himself up onto the raised bench. The oversized springs bounced beneath the seat.

Though taller than normal, Horra found no step to help her climb in, so she grasped hold of the side of the wagon and after a couple of attempts, she fumbled in, head over feet. Pidge squeaked, and Horra squealed to cover it up.

She should've made it a condition that he agreed to help her as well as keep her safe. An amateur mistake on her part.

Woodsly would've surely taken points off for that slip. Righting and dusting herself off, she sent Balk a withering glance and checked her pocket to be sure the seed was still safe. It was.

Without looking back at her, the bocan slapped the reins and the wagon wrenched forward, knocking her onto her back. She scrambled to keep hold of her sack and not squish the pudge wudgie any more than she had already.

The road they traveled was worn and rutted, and the wagon jerked her back and forth. After a few failed attempts at sitting up, Horra relented and lay on the rumbling floor of the cart. She adjusted the seed in her pocket so it wouldn't wear another bruise on her hip.

She closed her eyes, allowing the rocking motion and Pidge's cooing snores in her ear to lull her into a light sleep.

All too soon, the wagon slowed to a bumping stop. Horra flopped over and stood. Her body buzzed from the uneven path and all the jittering about. The forest around them was dark and imposing.

"Something's not right." Balk glanced around.

She spun in a circle, looking. "I don't see anything."

"My neck hairs don't lie."

"Can I sit up front? Your wagon's not comfortable." Being jostled around wasn't her idea of getting to Hobgoblin Pass safely.

He harrumphed at her. "You're a pampered princess, aren't you?"

Her spine stiffened. "Not as much as you'd think. Slide over." When he didn't move, she added, "please?"

The bocan let out a long groan. "Fine, but I'm not making small talk with you." He lifted her inelegantly out of the back and plunked her down on the seat.

The cloak was a tangle around her. She waded through,

disentangling herself so she didn't sit on a lump of fabric. "Do they not teach bocans manners?"

Balk's deadly gaze glinted. "This isn't high tea, princess." The wagon rocked as he shifted and snapped the reins. "Hold on and keep that cloak around you. I can't give you *safe passage* if you don't stay hidden."

Horra understood. It would be her fault if she got caught, and his promises would be done. She tucked the material around her, covering every inch except what she could see out of.

"So, what are you doing alone and off of your mountain?" Balk asked, his eyes on the ground where there wasn't an apparent path. High grasses swayed with the breeze and glowed dazzling with the silvery moonlight.

"Why were you skulking around Wester?" she countered.

He frowned. "You're not the only one in this kingdom being hunted."

Fear zinged through her veins. Was she in more danger now than before? "Who's hunting you?"

"The same being I'm hunting down. My daughter's murderer."

Horra wasn't sure if she should believe him, not until tears glistened in his eyes. Was he *crying*? Who knew bocans cried? "I—I'm sorry. What happened?"

"It's still new, sorry." He swiped at his eyes. "I don't know how it happened. I was off on a paid mission in the giant lands. By the time I got home, Floke had already been buried next to her mother, Glinn. No one could tell me what happened, only that she'd been attacked. Some sort of a spell they said. Turned her stiff like she was made of stone."

The pang of remembered loss made her nose sting with empathy. "That's terrible. If no one knows anything, how are you searching for the creature who did this? Do you know who it was?"

"Not for sure, but I have a hunch." He breathed hard. "I've seen a dark elf from time to time in my travels. Comes from the tainted forest on the edge of the elflands is my guess. Whenever he leaves a place, there's an unexplainable death. Something heinous. I've retraced the pubs I thought I saw him at and he's completely disappeared. I met with an elf informant tonight in the pub. Said there was another of his kind, a dangerous one who was expelled from the elflands."

They hit a small rise in the ground that didn't intimidate the horses but rattled the wagon. Horra held on desperately and held her breath until they were on smoother land. The bocan's idea of keeping her safe was vastly different from her version.

He continued, unfazed. "The Sylvan sliced off this elf's ears for doing dark magic. He lived in the Riven for a short while. Then he disappeared. Now I'm headed for that forest. It's not far from Hobgoblin's Pass. I'll drop you off and go searching for clues there."

Horra had heard of the Sylvan, the high elf council. Whatever this elf had done, it must've been bad. The wagon hit a rut and Horra jerked, unable to catch herself before she rolled across the seat and up against the mercenary. His arm stopped her from landing in his lap. "Careful there, princess. Might want to hold on."

Like she hadn't been? She didn't say it, though. She swallowed back her anger because she had questions about that elf. Maybe it was the hooded man from the castle. "I saw an elf at the Boar's Head. When he saw me, he yelled for the others."

Balk grunted. "My informant. He's running scared. Jumping at every shadow. And that much gold would turn anyone into a snitch. It turned my head until you pulled that dagger." He nodded at her.

She ground her teeth. "That poster is all lies."

He shrugged. "Doesn't matter, Princess. Money talks. Sweetly, usually. But in your case, not so sweet."

Her heart slammed in her chest at his admission. Had she worded their oath wrong? Was she safe with this bocan?

CHAPTER 17

Her mind raced to figure out if she'd made a mistake. The oath was solid, wasn't it? "If what you just said is true, how can I trust you now? What stops you from getting the dagger and then later turning me in?" They exited the dark thicket of trees and the moon shone dully on his tattooed scalp.

"You can't trust anyone. And if I were you, I wouldn't trust me either."

Again her mind spun with scenarios and different things she should've done differently. All sound around her dimmed as she went back over the oath they made over and over again.

Balk stared at her as if waiting for a reply.

"I'm sorry. Mudheadedness. What'd you say?" Horra shook herself internally. The oath was made. She'd just have to be more cautious moving forward.

"Look, you're safe, okay? I was telling you about my daughter, Floke." Balk's demeanor changed as he filled her in about his daughter's shining attributes.

An hour later, Horra yawned. She hadn't realized how

talkative mercenaries could be. Balk had raved on and on about the girl, but Horra's courtesy was near its end. She interrupted him mid-sentence. "She sounds like a great goblin. I wish I could help you, but I'm on my own quest."

His gaze was curious. "And what quest would that be?"

Her mind raced. Should she tell him? Civil conversation or not, he'd told her earlier not to trust him. "There was a coup at Nomans Castle. There were fairies and some gaunt guy wearing a cape. They got my father and now they're after me."

Balk laughed. "Fairies, you say? The creatures full of floaty and sparkly magic. What'd they do? Blow some glitter at the king and he just disappeared?"

She stared at him, her cheeks heating. She shouldn't have said anything. Just should've made up a tale like she was running away. He might've believed that.

"You're serious, aren't you?" Surprise crept across his scarred face. He rubbed his bald head.

"It was an unexpected visit. No warning. They just showed up. By the time the evening was over, the hobgoblins were acting crazy, a black-caped man tried to capture me, and my father was missing." She thought about telling him about Woodsly's seed, but it, like the dagger, was priceless. She didn't trust him enough to confide that.

Balk stared at her. "You mentioned a man wearing a black cape. Did he play strange music by chance?"

She worked to keep the eagerness out of her voice. It had to be the same guy. "Tinkly, awful music. Yes, why?"

"Because, Princess, the elf I'm searching for uses music to manipulate other creatures."

She knew it! They rode for a while in silence, both deep in thought. Horra understood her history. The first Erlking was a rogue elf. Woodsly's declaration of the second coming of the Erlking turned her bones to water. She'd believed him. Her old instructor didn't lie. But it hadn't been quite as real until Balk confirmed what she already believed. She plucked mindlessly at the worn cape with her claws.

The air grew heavy. Blue light glittered among the treetops behind them. Balk snapped the reins. "Get in back, Princess."

Horra didn't hesitate to crawl over the back of the seat and into the shallow bed. She crouched with the cloak covering her, head to toe. Her heaving breath was warm inside the heavy fabric, but she dared not pull it down.

"Whoa there, beasts." Muscles in Balk's arms bulged as he struggled to control the Stempners. True to their reputation, they were easily spooked.

Above Horra, something whizzed by, moving the cape. Then a thunk. An arrow? No, a magic spell. "What's happening?" she yelled to be heard above the noise of the wagon and the horse's hooves. She peeked at the bocan.

"Fairies. If you value your life, Princess, be quiet!" he hissed at her. In a quick movement, Balk shifted his feet.

Immediately, the boards beneath Horra gave way, and she fell. Before she could catch her breath, it was knocked out of her as she dropped into a holding box. Pidge squawked and fluttered out of her hood.

The boards above her closed silently. It reminded her of the iron locks in the castle. Curious, she ran her claws across the crude hold for a trigger or a lever that might help aid in an escape but found none. Fear settled into a ball in her gut as the cart slowed, though Balk kept screaming at the horses to keep going. She knew it wasn't like the beasts to slow down during trouble. They should be running for the hills at their top speed.

Dread kept her silent.

The wagon stopped abruptly and she rolled against the back of the hold box. Pidge scrambled across her face, tangling in her hair.

There was a muffled argument, but the words were spoken so fast she couldn't understand them. A light flashed through the cracks of the boards above her. Horra grabbed Pidge in case they heard her fluttering around, letting her go once the illumination disappeared. More angry words were exchanged. A crunch and the bocan cried out in pain, followed immediately by a hefty thump rattling the boards above her.

Flipping over to her belly, her hand struck a hard, cold surface. Digging through the fabric, she found the object and pulled it out. It was too dark to see clearly, even with her troll night vision, but it cut her finger. Avoiding the sharp edge, she carefully ran her hand up the item with its inset gems, and engraved symbols, landing on the unique pommel end. She'd held this particular weapon a hundred times before. Her hand closed around the familiar metal handle of her mother's dagger.

But—how?

Panic grew until it oozed from her hide in cold sweat. The oath was broken and magic had returned the dagger to her. It was either because the bocan was dead or was now unable to complete his pledge. She didn't like either option. Especially if fairies were involved.

Pidge flounced around the small space, possibly sensing Horra's alarm. "Don't worry, girl. I'll get us out of here," she whispered.

Horra wedged the dagger into the cracks between the wooden boards, but she couldn't pry them apart. The horses whinnied and stomped their massive hooves, impatient as usual. Magic flowed, rolling over her and then disappearing.

She shifted and tried to find purchase in between the slats on the bottom of the box. She shifted again to the other side, causing Pidge to flitter out of the way. The seed dug into her side, but she ignored that pain. After four tries, one board loosened. She frantically dug around with the blade. Her hands stung with cuts, but she didn't stop.

Chanting from a feminine voice washed over her. The cart lurched, and the horses took off again, this time with a different, vigorous fervor.

Her bones rattled, but she kept prying. The board gave way, and weeds and twigs brushed by the spot. The opening was too small for her to climb through. There wasn't enough room to try to dig another board loose, and she didn't want to waste any more time in a runaway cart being driven by someone she didn't know.

Blue light streaked and the cart tilted upwards.

Hurrying, she stuck the dagger inside the knapsack and groped for the bag holding the giant's food. She dug through, found the candy, and ate a piece.

Stomach cramping, she grabbed the pudge wudgie and the knapsack. In seconds she grew smaller, giving her more room to move. She rolled over to the opening.

Cold blue light flickered and the cart lifted but fell against the ground again.

The knapsack got stuck on a loose nail as she fell, and Horra dangled from the wagon with one arm in the air holding the knapsack strap and the bag of candy, and the other holding on to a squirming bird.

The blue light took hold and the wagon shifted into the air.

"Stop moving, Pidge, or I'll lose you."

The fabric of the sack ripped. Pieces of the cookie dropped out of the bag. Horra opened her mouth wide and caught a couple of crumbs. She swallowed and waited. Her body tingled and the knapsack rip, rip, ripped as she grew.

Then they were tumbling to the ground as the wagon flew off, sailing along the trees and into the moonlit sky.

CHAPTER 18

Pidge's wings fluttered free of Horra's hand, and the bird uttered an angry screech. Horra glanced around at the dark edge of the forest, made darker by an eerily lit path running through the trees and sparkling into the sky. "Sorry, Pidge."

The bird fluffed her feathers and pecked at the glowing residue on the ground.

The forest surrounding them was dotted with curving, twisted trees. The scent of this wood was different than the crisp pine of the mountains. It was earthier and held a tang of rotting leaves.

They needed to move in case the fairy realized she was gone. Had they known she was on board? Balk had mentioned she wasn't the only one being hunted.

Though talking with the bocan had been a nice change, she was glad to have her mother's dagger returned. She prayed he was safe, whatever happened to him. Even mercenaries didn't deserve to have fairies kidnap them.

Horra's feet tangled in the cloak and she rolled around to

get loose. Although it might hide her better than her vapid vestra jacket, it was bulky and tripped her. There was no room in her knapsack for it, so she wadded it up and tucked it into the hollow of a large tree. She smoothed her unruly hair back and pulled the hood over it. Pidge toddled behind her, pecking at the glowing foliage.

Though she'd read about fairy paths, she'd never actually seen one. It was creepier in real life. Horra touched the path, which glowed with frigid magic. Her claw tingled like she'd laid on it wrong for too long. Her books mentioned the brighter the path was, the stronger it was. She glanced up at the dark sky. This one had to be pretty strong. One a princess or a queen could conjure? She shook the magic residue off.

Balk had been headed for Hobgoblin's Pass. That was a main road that would take her close to the Weald. She needed to find it.

Whoever their attackers were, they had to have known she was in the wagon. It didn't fit that the fairies would be after Balk. He had no fight with them and thought they were harmless. She was too tired to contemplate everything, and she needed to keep moving.

After another dose of the cookie, she walked hurriedly back the way the wagon had come, which she had no trouble finding thanks to the halting, glowing path. How were the fairies constantly a step behind her? Balk had been scared for one moment when she'd crawled to the seat. Could it have been them he sensed?

Was there some sort of beacon on her, a tracking device? Lately, in court, it had been uncovered that the dwarfs had been using fake, charmed gems to find who'd been stealing from their Dunder Mound Caverns. Several spriggans were caught when the gems exploded, giving them weltering, painful rashes which covered their crusty bodies. They'd run from wherever they were, screaming about being burned alive.

Pidge raced off after something in the brush ahead of them, squealing with delight once she captured her prey. Horra's stomach grumbled. The only edible things she had would make her bigger or smaller, neither of which appealed to her at the moment.

Why couldn't Woodsly have taught her how to hunt beyond learning how to hit a target with an arrow? Oh, she had been versed in wild edibles in their Horticulture class, but to hunt and trap were not taught until the year before she would become queen.

A sweet odor came from a cluster of bushes to her left. Chokeberries! She plucked a handful of fruit, and just as she was going to toss them in her mouth, Pidge swooped in and gulped them down.

"Hey! Those weren't yours. Go chase your measly mice or I'll shrink you so much you won't be able to eat them." Horra shooed the bird away. The bird flew a few yards and squawked. Horra picked and ate the berries in a hurry.

She gathered the final remaining berries from the bush, stuffing them in the pocket with Woodsly's seed. Pidge moved a few steps closer at one point but stopped when Horra turned to face her pet. She'd never actually punished the pudge wudgie. Not really. She'd gotten cross with the bird, yes. But she'd never raised a hand to hurt her. Horra had never been this tired, hungry, and hunted before. Guilt flooded her. She didn't like what it was doing to her. They needed to get to the Weald.

"C'mon, Pidge." Horra tossed the bird a berry, a sort of apology, and ate the others one by one out of her pocket so Pidge didn't get any more ideas of stealing them. Chokeberries had been one of her and her mother's favorites. They'd had them when they'd taken their journey to Norrow Lake to make their wishes. It had been the last time she'd eaten them until now. Would the memories never stop being painful?

The sun was starting to rise when they reached a rutted road. Horra's shoulders drooped in exhaustion. She stuck to the forest's edge along the road until she came to a spot where the road's ditch dipped into a deep ravine.

She had one berry left. "Here, girl." The berry gleamed a deep purplish-black in the sunlight. She tucked it into the back of her hoodie and Pidge dodged into the coat to get it, nestling down against Horra's neck once it was eaten.

Several groups of people, horses, and buggies traveled the road. Some had animals tagging along, others had wares to sell. While a few others walked, the majority had wagons or trailers full of items. It was busy, almost alarmingly so, as winter was coming soon and everyone wanted to get the final sales in before the weather slowed things down.

Horra clung to the edges and kept her head down. Heavy clops of a horse behind her made her move closer to the side for safety. However, the beast strode close enough to knock her sideways into the bramble along the ditch. She landed on her bottom with an 'oof.' Her hood fell, and a sleeping Pidge rolled into the brown grass.

The black stallion's tail whipped as she scowled. "There's more than enough room on this road, you stupid beast!"

The hoofbeats slowed to a stop far enough around a bend in the road that Horra could hear but not see them. It was quite possible whoever it was had heard what she said. She grabbed Pidge, shoved her back in her hood, and ducked into the shaded forest. Here the leaves were damp and slick, and Horra slipped down the side of a hill. Hoofbeats stopped above her, right at the spot she'd been standing.

That was too close! She needed to find another route that wasn't so clogged with travelers. She sat and waited to calm herself while the horse cantered away, and then waited some more before getting up and moving deeper into the forest. Less sunlight filtered through the trees the further in she traveled.

Horra sneezed and her nose stuffed up. Air thickened with the pungent scent of rot and decay. And—she sniffed stuffily—poison? The bottoms of the trees along the area were covered with a beard of sphagnum, hornwort, and a black, dusty fungus. Slime covered the tips of her boots and soaked her pant legs up to her knees. Her backside was already damp from her slide down the hill, and she shivered against a cool breeze.

She needed to get back in the sun and away from the blight around her, or she could grow ill or catch the crud. The illness that robbed her mother of her life. Nothing could get rid of the crud. Not even a rare magical wish.

Horra rushed, clutching the hood tight around her nose and mouth, hoping she didn't suffocate the pudge wudgie, toward a brighter area. Several times she stumbled over fallen limbs and uneven ground, scraping her arms and face. Once she fell, mouth open as she screamed, and received a mouthful of vile-tasting lichen. Her stomach clenched and she vomited into the weeds before staggering back to her feet and running out of the blighted thicket. Sunlight glittered ahead, and she finally arrived at a tiny wagon trail cutting through the forest.

Sunlight warmed her after she dropped the hood away from her face. Pidge fluttered free, a bit disoriented, but fine nonetheless. Horra drug in deep cleansing breaths, willing away any contaminated spores she might have ingested and coughed. She gagged once more and fell to the ground, grateful to have gotten out of the poisoned woods.

Drenched to the point of dripping mire, Horra removed her hoodie, pants, and boots. She dug out the seed and bags and shoved them into the knapsack. Luckily the wool socks kept her claws from getting wet, so she kept those on to ward off the chill that had sunk deep into her bones.

She needed a fire. Keeping the poison forest behind her, she gathered several sticks and brush and piled them in a clear spot. She lifted her right claw to start the fire.

"I wouldn't draw attention to myself if I were you." A voice like two sticks rubbing against each other called out.

Startled, Horra glanced around, aware she wore only her socks, underthings, and shirt. She hugged an arm around her middle. "Woodsly?" she called out, worried she was hallucinating.

"Panicking and yelling are not helping you at this point, troll princess." The voice became louder, more of a clacking sound.

She swung around, catching a glance at Pidge, who was digging at a worm in the dirt not far away. Close enough to grab and run. "I wouldn't yell if I knew who I was talking with. How do you know who I am?"

A creaking groan resonated to her left. It was a sound she remembered Woodsly making from time to time. She turned to face a gnarled, old tree. Were they hiding behind it?

Horra grabbed the biggest limb she'd gathered and held it up. "Show yourself."

The forest grew silent as if it were placed under a bowl. Bark on the side of the tree split open and shifted. Eyes indented, a large, bulbous nose formed, and a beard took shape. Where Woodsly had been all smooth bark, this face was creased and rough.

"Greetings, Princess."

CHAPTER 19

Horra stepped back. "Wha—who are you?"

"I'm Kryk, a rood of the forest." His *clackity* words reminded Horra of Woodsly's voice. Longing ached inside her. If only she could speak with him once more.

Horra recalled Woodsly's history lessons about how the roods had helped her grandmother, Queen Petra, win the War of the Warts. Roods were holy and benevolent, helping those they deemed worthy. "I didn't know there were still roods around."

"Ah, yes. We're always around." Two branches moved and clasped limbs in front of the tree like it had hands. "Surely your instructor, Sir Woodsly, told you about us."

Sir? "He mentioned roods, yes. Before—" She pulled the seed from her knapsack and rubbed at a smudge of black mold that must've come from her journey through the poisoned forest. The smudge disappeared, leaving behind a dark mark on the shell. She rubbed the seed harder, but it didn't make the mark go away. Had the poison affected the seed? Woodsley would be so disappointed in her.

"That is why I'm here, though I was delayed. The spirits were summoned when Woodsly chose to revert his life magic to a seed. Though there used to be dozens, Woodsly was the last great druid warrior. So, I've come to help guide you to bring the seed to the Weald. News has traveled through our roots that you are being watched, sought by an evil that would destroy us all," Kryk said.

Chills raced across Horra's hide. It was essentially the same thing Balk told her. "Is it the Erlking? They have my father. Why are they after me, too?"

"Revenge, Princess. On your father, yes. But more importantly on you."

Horra clutched the seed tight. "Why me? I've never hurt anyone or anything."

Kryk's face twisted, and he stroked his bark beard with one of his limb hands. "It has nothing to do with you and everything to do with your grandmother. Queen Petra overpowered the first Erlking in the War of the Warts. Now another Erlking has risen, and he seeks revenge against you because of that loss. He has already mesmerized the fairies, who were the troll's biggest allies in the war. He uses a special kind of mind control on them and other creatures to track you, using them to bring you to him. Once he has you, your kingdom, he can take over the rest of the Wilden Lands."

"But why? Why is the Erlking trying to take over everything?" Frustrated, Horra placed the seed back in the sack.

Kryk's limbs shrugged like shoulders. "Why do any of us do what we do? For good or ill we all must choose how we react to what happens to us in life. Do we seek revenge or forgiveness? It's all up to who you are deep inside because we all have the power of good or evil in our hearts." He pointed to her, poking the spot above her heart with a twig finger.

Horra studied the wizened wooden face. "And who am I?"

"That, Princess, is up to you to decide." Kryk glanced up and peered behind her. "We are running out of time. I can only suspend this moment for so long." One arm reached up into some branches stretching above them. "Take this and put it on. It will protect you on your journey." Kryk held out something that resembled a cloak made of wood. It was carved with a pattern of symbols and marks she didn't recognize.

"Um—"

"This woodencloak is armor from the Great Yew Tree at the center of the Weald. It is carved with magical spells of protection and blessings in ancient druid languages. You will need it to get to the Weald unharmed and in time to replant the seed. Travel down the path in this direction. We will be close by, offering what help we can. But you must hurry—"

Before Horra could blink, the stillness was broken. Time rushed in with the wind and blew her a step back into Pidge who was still scavenging for bugs. She glanced around. The face on the tree was gone, but the cloak remained suspended, hanging from the tree's limb, which was pointing down the road.

A rumbling sounded from afar. Horra jerked her jacket off and grabbed the woodencloak. Though she was expecting splinters and hardwood, it was pliable like the vapid vestra fabric. It creaked and shrank to fit her, settling over her head and spreading down the length of her arms and legs in a barkish hide.

Great. She looked like Woodsly now. The only thing she needed was a nubby tail. Horra put her boots back on.

The rumbling sounded louder.

She shoved everything back into the knapsack, making sure the seed was still there and tucked Pidge in her hood.

A moment later, a buggy rattled behind her on a curve along the road. Horra stepped behind the tree Kryk occupied a moment before.

A peddler drove a colorful wagon with all kinds of objects dangling from metal hooks across the exterior. There were hammers, pots and pans, a couple of saws, and a few furs wagging back and forth with the motion of the wagon.

There on the back was a boggret, an uncannily large, brownish bog rat. It sat on the backboard and chewed on a hanging fur hide. Its beady eyes scanned the area, and then it turned away.

Pidge shifted against her neck, scenting either the critter or the hide, no doubt. "Not now, girl. We can't get caught, especially if he just came from that last town we were in." Horra pulled the hood tight, trapping the bird before it could fly away, and waited several minutes before she stepped out and continued down the path in the direction Kryk pointed.

Half a day later she came to a wooden sign on the side of the road: *Hobgoblin Pass 30 miles ahead.*

Thirty miles? She wasn't sure if she could go thirty more feet.

Horra shifted the knapsack from one shoulder to the other. Though it was smaller, it was beginning to weigh her down, making her shoulders ache more. Sun, along with her pace, had kept her soaked with sweat. Her clawed feet, which rarely wore shoes, had begun to form blisters.

She needed to sleep as much as she needed food. And water. The forest was fairly dense here, the trees were no longer bent and curvy, but tall and sturdy. If she could find a sheltered, open spot, she'd put the tent up.

That decided, Horra trudged into the woods, instantly

cooling with the dappled shade the bare limbs afforded. It sloped and she slid down the leafy incline. Farther in, she found a small, trickling stream just big enough to wash in and drink from.

"Here, Pidge." She removed the cloak and let the bird fly down to the stream. They both drank. Horra rubbed the cool water across her too-warm hide and soaked her aching toes in the stream.

Pidge took off after another unsuspecting varmint, flying this way and that, stopping only to gulp down whatever she'd caught.

Not far from the stream where Horra rested stood a grand oak tree. At the tree's base grew a cluster of frond-tailed mushrooms. She plucked one and sniffed it before popping it in her mouth.

Her taste buds sang with delight.

When she'd had her fill and added the rest to her knapsack for later, she scouted for a place to pitch the tent and found one between two large trees on a hill overlooking a large dale. There below spread hobgoblin farmland. Here, she could spy out in every direction and remain hidden. The sky on the horizon darkened. She caught the scent of a storm on the breeze. She needed to hurry.

Using her Wandering Wilderness skills, she laid a bed of fallen leaves before pitching the tent, used the stream and some rocks to wash herself and her clothes, and built a fire.

By the time the fire was in embers, she was ready to collapse. Her wet clothes were hung inside the tent and she gathered the heated stones from the fire to keep them warm during the night.

Using a couple of the torentula eggs she'd gathered from the giant's house, she lured Pidge into the tent. She was asleep almost before she could close her eyes.

CHAPTER 20

Pidge shivered beside her neck when Horra woke up inside the dark tent. Snow pellets *tick, tick, ticked* against the fabric. However, it was warm inside the tent, thanks to the added leaves. She sat up and tried to gather her wits.

Wind whistled and the wyvern hide ruffled above them. Horra crawled over to open it and peek outside. Snowy sleet came down in sheets across the hillside and rushed across the valley below. The trees had a glittering icy coat, and snow covered the leaves on the ground. The wind whipped up a blast of snow pellets and threw them her way. Horra sealed up the tent in time to miss getting hit in the face by them.

The storm was worse than Horra thought it would be. They weren't going anywhere for a while. She twisted the fabric of her shirt over her fingers. All of her Wandering Wilderness skills would be called upon to stay warm during this icy blast. If only they could build a fire inside the tent, but not only would it be foolish, she also hadn't collected any sticks and wood.

She touched the trousers hung by the opening. They were stiff, but dry enough to put on and stay warm, so she slipped them on. She did the same with the tunic, adding the vapid vestra jacket on top. She took the woodencloak and stuck it beside the mattress for Pidge to bed down. Possibly she should've kept the bocan's cloak, but there was no way she would've made it through the poisoned forest with it.

Horra sighed. She hadn't thought she'd get stuck in a winter blast. She took two of the mushrooms she'd picked and ate them. They made her thirsty, which gave her an idea. She dumped the last torentula eggs out of the bag for Pidge, and opened the tent so she could fill it full of snow.

Pidge probably had had enough the past few days while they'd been out on the run, but Horra hadn't eaten much that didn't shrink her or make her larger. She'd need to conserve the mushrooms. There's no way she'd use the giant's food unless it was an emergency.

Pidge gobbled the eggs up before Horra slushed the bag clean, and filled it with snow. With a flick of her claws, she produced a flame on her clawtips, and instead of letting it die like when she lit the torches in the castle, she held it in place to melt the snow. She drank most of it and let Pidge have the rest.

She put the flame to one of the stones until her clawed nail burned out. She tucked it between her and Pidge to help ward off the chill.

Wind whipped frantically outside of the tent, so she lay back down to nap. Pidge circled a spot inside the cloak, fluffed her feathers, and settled down next to the heated stone.

When Horra woke up again, she was anxious to get moving. However, the snow was still falling, and this time it was heavy and thick. Hazy sunlight radiated through the tent's wyvern scales. After sitting around twiddling her claws, Horra dug the Medicinal Curse Book out. Maybe she'd find something important if she read it. She started at a note to the reader penned by the druid authors.

Good and evil fight for dominance in this magical realm and across realms both seen and unseen—known and unknown. Because everything has a purpose, there will always be those who oppose that purpose and seek to establish self as the purpose, at least until the final age when darkness will be no more, praise the Creature God. Until then, those who walk by light magic must arm themselves with the tools needed to fight and protect themselves from dark magic users. This book with its counterspells and protections has been compiled by the best scholars and druid-born wielders since the beginning of the forest age. Each spell has been tested and the results, when used with the right motivations, are guaranteed. Use them wisely.

Boring! Horra flipped through the illustrated pages, skimming over protective charms and counter-potions. Most of the ingredients and methods she'd heard about or learned from Woodsly. It was all fairly basic until she got to the section on mesmerization.

"Here we are, Pidge." She read aloud, "'symptoms of someone trying to mesmerize you: One: sudden sleepiness for no apparent reason. Two: forced thoughts. Thoughts that are not your own overtake you, making you act in a manner that is out of character.'"

She stopped reading, excited and dismayed at the same time. "That's what that guy was doing to me. Something pressed on my mind in the kitchen! I didn't think trolls could be mesmerized, though."

Horra read on, "'three: dancing. If you have an uncontrollable impulse to dance without end.' Huh. I hate dancing."

Pidge chirped drowsily at her.

"'Four: weighted air. When the air around you becomes

murky and makes it hard to breathe or move.' So, that's what that was." Not that she hadn't known it was magic, just not the purpose exactly. "'Five: sudden dizziness. Six: levitation.'" Horra slapped the book. Just the thought of hovering without any control made shivers crawl across her hide. "'Seven: blackouts. When you have not imbibed in drink or silly weed and you wake without remembering the last few hours to days, you may have been mesmerized.'"

Horra blanched. "That's awful!" She followed her claw down to the last notes, "'Blackouts are tricky! You will have to do a full reversal to undo the spell. Warning: effects from the reversal may be permanent. Mesmerization takes many forms: spoken word, charmed object, spiked food or drink, or repeated incantations.'"

Horra laughed. "Well, if repeated incantations cause mesmerization, Woodsly failed miserably with his etiquette lessons."

Pidge tucked her beak under her wing and closed her golden eyes

"I thought that was funny. Anyway, it says certain creatures are more susceptible to mesmerization." She flipped to chapter twenty when the book referred her to protective charms, counter-spells, and reversals.

There she found a long list of ingredients and numerous steps needed for the protection and unmesmerization potion, but nothing exotic or unusual.

Horra then paged over to the creature list. "Huh, good thing I'm a royal girl troll, Pidge. We are the least likely of all the Wilden creatures to become mesmerized because of our contrary nature. Contrary nature?" She slammed the book shut with a frown. "Billy goats! I'm not contrary at all."

However, if her father and the others were all mesmerized

... she shivered at more than just the whining wind outside of the tent.

Horra dug out the last of the mushrooms, breaking off small pieces to feed Pidge, and repeated the snow-to-water nourishment. When her eyes crossed and were unable to read and the boredom became too much, Horra lay down to rest again.

When she woke next, the wind had died down, but it was dark. How many days had passed? She was unsure. It could only have been two or possibly three.

Horra peeked outside the opening. The tent was covered halfway up and weighted down with snow. No wonder it was warmer this time waking up. They were insulated.

The moon rose in the east, spreading silver light across the land.

She sealed the tent back up and prepared to pack when her hide tingled like fizz and the air in the tent thickened.

Muted tinkling notes filtered through the tent.

CHAPTER 21

Horra stilled, waiting. The top of the tent glittered with flashing lights through the spots not covered with snow. Horra was beginning to despise piskies. The tinkling notes coalesced into an annoying tune.

Pidge stood and walked toward the sound.

Horra grabbed her, holding her beak shut gently to keep the bird from making any noise. She prayed silently that whatever was outside would pass quickly. Time dragged on. Voices similar to the one from her failed wagon ride came from outside the tent. Somewhere too close for comfort.

Her knapsack sat at her right while the woodencloak lay by the sleeping bag. Horra hoped the snow and the camouflaging quality of the tent would fool anyone searching for her, but since they were so close, she had doubts.

She should have searched in the Medicinal Curse Book for information about magical trackers or how to become invisible.

The voices grew louder, and snow outside of the tent crunched. Horra held her breath. After a short period, the voices drifted away and the tinkling music faded to nothing. Pidge struggled in her claws, and she let the bird down. She teetered to the corner of the tent away from her, chirped angrily, and fluffed her feathers.

Horra flopped back down. "Sorry, girl. Better smashed and alive than dead."

How long would she need to wait before she could pack up without being caught? From what she could tell, there had been at least three creatures talking, so there were too many for her to take on by herself. She didn't want to wait for daytime, but she might have to now to be safe.

Time passed slowly as Horra waited, trying to be patient. She'd had too much sleep already, so she checked the book for information on trackers, but there wasn't any, not under any heading, nor anywhere she scan-read through. Maybe it was too old for that kind of magic?

Eventually, she could stand it no longer. She checked to make sure everything was in the knapsack, deflated the mattress, and donned the woodencloak before coaxing Pidge into her hood with a crumb of dried mushroom. Her stomach clenched just thinking about food.

Stone held in her hand, she peeked her head out of the tent. When nothing moved, she brushed away the snow as she stepped out. Indentations of where someone had traveled by sleigh and walked around the hilltop were within a rock's throw from the tent. Footprints dotted a couple of areas before the wagon trail led left, away from where she'd been headed, thankfully.

It took some effort, and a lot of sinking into the deep snow, but she dug out the stakes, folded the tent back up, and tucked it into the sack. It would be wet for the next use, but it couldn't be helped.

She shoveled handful after handful of snow over the leafy square left behind from her tent. The wind blowing the snow around would cover what she didn't.

Though cold, Horra had worked up a sweat. She gazed down the hill to the valley below. Moonlight on the untouched snow glistened much like the fairies, all perky and pretty. Horra frowned. The snow was probably deeper the farther down she'd travel. She recalled one winter exercise where Woodsly had her fashion her own snowshoes and sled. She'd loved it so much that she created her own from then on. Her heart twisted and she longed for the days when she was carefree and not hunted or running. The cold made her nose run.

Sniffing and running her sleeve across her nose, she studied the trees around her and chose some pliable limbs to bend and weave into something resembling a snowshoe. The sled would be harder.

One large tree had thick, loose bark. She pried until her claws were sore but got it off in a big enough chunk that she could sit and slide down the hill.

She tied the roundish snowshoes onto her boots, using her long bootstrings, and dropped the bark at the edge of the hill. With Pidge safely tucked in her hood, Horra sat down, adjusted the knapsack in her lap, and with a couple of sturdy limbs she used as poles, she pushed off.

The snow was light and fluffy, perfect for her to sink into and for the makeshift sled to gather speed on the way down. She leaned back and forth to avoid trees or mounds of earth, though a couple scraped the bottom of the bark.

Cold air nipped at her face, freezing the snot dripping from her nose. She bit back a squeal of delight. Her hood rippled, and Pidge stuck her head out. She couldn't lift a claw to stop her, and, before Horra could react, the pudge wudgie darted off into the air with an equally gleeful screech. She couldn't blame her. It was the perfect night to go sledding.

All too soon, her trip ended. Pidge circled the sky above her. Horra's cheeks were numb and her hair askew, but it had been glorious sailing over the snow with the air rushing through her hair. It energized her enough to hustle through the valley, hoping and praying her hunters hadn't seen her wild ride.

The snowshoes slish-slushed through the snow. Horra kept a close watch in case any flashing lights popped up. But only the glorious silver moonlight reflected in the glittering landscape. Twice, she stopped and checked the now-working compass for south-southeast, in the direction Kryk had pointed her.

A couple of times, she'd lost Pidge along the way, only to have her reappear again looking quite pleased with herself. Horra didn't know how the bird did it since all of the other wildlife had disappeared, probably hibernating like smart creatures. But they didn't call pudge wudgies master hunters for no reason.

At least one of us is getting dinner.

By the time Horra found what appeared to be a road, the moon was creeping lower in the sky. Round huts dotted the sleeping countryside, and smoky scents of dying fires filled the crisp air. The fires reminded her of food, and food made her stomach gurgle.

She whistled. "C'mon, girl. Can't have someone finding you and keeping you for their pet." Pidge circled twice more before flying down to land on her shoulder. With a flick, Horra covered her head with the hood.

Several yards away was an enormous oak tree on the side of the road creaking and swaying as if waving at her. She hesitated before shoeing over to it. "Kryk?"

The tree stilled, and so did Horra.

Tinkling notes carried across the frosty air seconds before five piskies floated down the road. The miniature fairy's wings shone with a golden radiance, hiding their appearance behind their brightness and reflecting like twinkling stars on the snow.

The two mammoth Stempners pulled the bocan's wagon behind them, making deep impressions in the snow as they traveled. A worq drove the steeds, another sat beside him trying to play the same kind of weird pan flute instrument the Erlking had used, but failing miserably in his attempts. It wasn't a song, but a group of off-key notes that rang wrong.

Horra recalled her lessons on worqs. They were the aberrant offspring of orqs and witches, both of which had been slaughtered almost to extinction by the first Druid Gathering after the Witchling Wars ages ago. The half-breed descendants were a scourge to any land they had the misfortune to settle in. They had taken over swamplands her forefathers had deserted when Oddar was formed. Since then, that had become a dangerous place to live.

A third hooded figure sat in the back with a quiver filled with arrows and a bow hung across their chest and displaying Oddar's coat of arms. A sword strapped to their belt had familiar hilts as well. They—he yelled at the other two in the front.

Shock rocketed through her as she recognized the voice and she slapped a hand over her mouth.

It was her classmate Torren. Why would he betray them in this way? Was he mesmerized?

The wagon stopped just past where she'd shoed off the road. She realized why she didn't recognize the language before. It was worqen.

Torren got out and circled the wagon, the piskies following him. It was the same wide shoulders, messy hair, and green, warty face she'd known since infancy. He turned and looked right at Horra.

CHAPTER 22

Horra's knees trembled. An ugly, menacing expression twisted Torren's face. His green brows were furrowed and a scowl replaced his usual easy smile. She couldn't see if his eyes were glazed.

Hot pain seared her heart as a voice inside her head reminded her that he could be under the Erlking's spell. She tried to get a better look at his face, but he turned this way and that in such a way she couldn't see clearly. He didn't look distracted. He wasn't dancing or floating.

Questions spun through her mind. His glance finally strayed to where she stood again. She stiffened, her lungs closing up, waiting for Torren to give her away, but he appeared to look right through her.

The woodencloak was working. But that realization was dampened by the fact her classmate was either under a thrall or was a traitor. She couldn't stop the sting of betrayal, no matter what the cause.

He walked around the front of the Stempners. The horses jerked and whinnied away from him, and the worq driver fought to keep control of the animals. Her father always told her never to walk in front of these particular animals. Torren should've known that, but he was oblivious to the horses as he made his way to the back.

He glanced her direction again, almost as if he sensed her, but there was no reaction. Whatever charms were on the woodencloak, they were powerful. The worqs snarled something at him and laughed. Torren snipped out a response and leaped easily into the back of the wagon.

Torren knew worqen language? They weren't taught that language. How had he learned it? Especially since he'd failed in goblin, hobgoblin slang, and dwarfen languages. All were loads easier than the twisted consonants of the worqen dialect.

With a grunt, the driver slapped the reins, and they took off with the piskies following them.

Horra let her legs go slack and slumped into the snow. It took several minutes before she was able to breathe normally. Tears streaked icy paths down her cheeks. She smashed them off with her sleeve and leaned her head against the tree.

"*Good work, Princess. Don't lose heart. The Weald is not far now.*" A wooden, *clackity* voice spoke in her mind.

"Is ... is Torren working with the Erlking? Has he betrayed our kingdom?" she asked.

"*Who can fully know the motives of another? It would be like trying to slice a hair in half with a sword.*"

She sat up and the voice disappeared. "Well, that was helpful." Anger fueled her sarcasm. In her heart, though, she knew the rood was probably right. Her body shook. Torren's betrayal hurt more than she wanted to admit. How many more of her subjects were doing the Erlking's bidding?

Horra made sure the road was clear before snow-shoeing back over to it. Her stomach pinched painfully. What she wouldn't give for some three-weed salad or roast swamp swine now. Before that last dinner, she'd never given hunger much thought. She'd need to get some food soon or she wouldn't be able to keep up her strength.

The sky turned pink and then orange until the sun's bright light dashed the darkness away. Horra had passed several hobgoblin houses and spied an area thick with cottages and buildings. She prayed that she'd make it through without being recognized.

Or seeing Torren again.

She passed by one cottage close to the road. Livestock in the pens called out to her, probably hoping for some oats or hay.

A goblin farmer came out with a bucketful of ashes. Horra stepped off the road and stood still, waiting for him to return inside.

Ash dirtied the pristine snow where it landed. The farmer glanced up at her and frowned. Horra's heart skipped a beat.

"Where'd that tree come from?"

Tree? Is that what she looked like? She was too afraid to move and see.

"Did you say something, Prack?" A woman joined the man.

"Where'd that tree come from?" He pointed at Horra. She stood still, waiting for them to recognize her. She held her breath.

"You're losing it, you old hobgoblin. That tree's been there for years." She took his bucket and returned inside.

The farmer scratched his bald head. He yelled through the barn door. "Nope. It hasn't. It could be Arbold playing tricks on us again." He rubbed his bulbous nose, never taking his eyes off Horra. "Where'd I put that ax?"

He turned to look for the tool and Horra rushed away, snow flying as she moved as fast as the snowshoes allowed.

A town came into sight not far down the road. A steeple spire poked above all of the other cottages. Creatures moved around, having awoken from a cold night's rest. Pregnant clouds inched across the faded blue sky.

Past several farms and isolated cottages, another village spread out in the valley. This hamlet had a board of announcements at the entrance. The sign read: *Welcome to Bough Valley, entryway to Hobgoblin Pass.*

Her wanted poster with a picture of her on it was curled and wet from the snowfall. Horra ripped it off and tore it into soggy pieces, tossing them into a snowy bush nearby.

A couple of hobgoblins with a small wagon full of wares traveled past her on the road into town. She didn't need the snowshoes any longer, so she bent down, untied them, and re-laced her boots. No one noticed her.

She glanced around at the other announcements and found one that shocked her more than her bounty poster had. It read:

Your attendance is cordially requested for the royal wedding of King Divitri Fyd to Queen Stella Toppenbottom on the second Moonday of the Silver Frost at sunset. A feast shall open the festivities, which will take place at Nomans Castle. No invitation required, but formal wear is necessary for entry.

Her father's signature was joined by the fairy queen's curly, swirly one. Horra stood, stunned. Her father was alive. He was alive! Thank the Creature God he was alive.

Then her heart thudded hard before freezing completely. He couldn't marry a fairy. Her kingdom would lose its blessing. And worse yet, it couldn't be undone until one of the parties was dead.

And fairies lived a long, long time. Much longer than trolls.

Pidge fluffed her feathers, tickling her neck, but she barely paid attention to it.

Horra's limbs were numb, not from the cold, but from the sheer shock. Her father was still alive and well. But he was to marry the friffity, floofy queen?

Over her cold, dead body!

Blood rushed to her head, and she was afraid she would throw up, though she had nothing in her gut to give up. Had her father completely lost his mind?

A fairy for a stepmother? Those two indolent princesses for half-sisters? Her gut clenched painfully. Never mind losing the blessing to her kingdom, she'd lose her mind if that were to happen.

It couldn't be. She wouldn't let it be.

It had to be magic! She wouldn't believe her father would agree to marry a fairy for any other reason. He'd be free to marry again if he wished, once she became queen. But if he married another creature now, he'd break two oaths. First, his oath of Queen's Champion that held Horra's place until she became queen. Unless her father died while trying to fulfill the oath, the penalty would itself be death. Second, the blood oath her foremothers made with the Creature God. He'd foresworn to uphold their law that no other race would rule over their kingdom while a royal troll still lived, or the Creature God's blessings and favor would be forfeit. Oddar would be no more.

Horra waited a couple of minutes, tapping her boot quietly but impatiently, for a hobgoblin to finish clearing the path and leave before she headed into town. Maybe she would be able to overhear information on the supposed wedding there.

She was careful to stand still each time she came upon someone. No one noticed her. A market with a couple of dozen stands had already opened when she made her way into the center of town. Luckily there were several other trees in the park area, so she would have no trouble standing and listening without being seen.

Several men came and went after buying goods. When the sun rose high enough to warm the day, women started to come out to shop. A rotund, rosy-cheeked hobgoblin was one of the first. She started at the bakery tables and worked her way over to a tailor.

"Morning, Marnell," the seller greeted the woman.

"Morning, Frilbus. Crazy business, the wedding, isn't it?" Marnell flipped through the folded cloths on his table. "I wouldn't consider going if there wasn't a reward. Do you have any silver silk?"

Frilbus shook his head and frowned. "I have a wonderful satin pink if you're interested. Queen Toppenbottom has requested only pastels for her most grand day. I was told the king himself will be wearing a flitterfly iridescent shade." His words were clipped, irritated.

Hope flared in her chest. Maybe not all of her trolldom had been mesmerized.

Marnell *tsked*. "Such a shame. Queen Terra was a wonderful queen. Do you recall she'd come here once or twice a year to check on us? She'd buy the last of our vegetables in the fall, and we always had enough money to last the winter." She grimaced. "Not so since. I can't imagine King Divitri doing this before the princess has her coronation. It's unheard of."

Pain crushed Horra's heart. She was heartened to know some creatures supported her and had common sense. Her mind returned to her benevolent mother. Horra had never realized to what extent. Her father, though fair and generous, hadn't taken up her mother's charitable legacy fully, and their kingdom's morale had taken a toll.

Frilbus nodded. "It's the talk of all the townships around. It is a disgrace. I refuse to attend, though I need to sell the fabric to those who will attend. The Hobgoblin Almanac forecasts a harsh winter. It's never wrong, you know." Frown lines deepened the hobgoblin's creased face.

"Of course, you're right." Marnell thunked the fabric down. "I hope the fairy queen trips on her way up the aisle."

Horra held back a snort. Lost in thought, she missed the last of their conversation, and not wanting to hear more, moved on to the food tables. The baker was first.

She held the hood tight to keep Pidge from dashing off after each new scent. The bird scratched and clawed at her neck in thanks.

She palmed a round loaf of thistleberry bread, sneaking a chunk of the bread to appease Pidge so she could gather more food. Beside the butcher, she grabbed a handful of blood sausages and a hunk of headcheese. She took only what she thought they could eat now and nothing more. Pledging silently to come back and make recompense, she made her way across the park to somewhere more private to eat.

"Hold on there. Where do you think you're going?" Horra turned in time to see a constable striding toward her.

CHAPTER 23

Horra stopped.

The constable stomped across the snow toward her.

She gulped. Her pockets were full of pilfered food. Her knapsack was on her back, so she couldn't reach any kind of weapon, though she doubted she'd draw the dagger anyway. She'd have to talk her way out of this like she had with the bocan. Her hands trembled as her mind scrambled for something plausible.

She was ready to give a lame explanation, but the constable strode past her. He left behind indentations in the snow where he stepped. She glanced behind her. There wasn't a trace of her steps anywhere. And when she glanced down at her body, she didn't see a tree, only the woodencloak with the symbols that spread to cover her fully.

The constable grabbed a small hobgoblin boy by the collar. "You're giving that back with an apology, Yocun."

The boy held a yellow ribbon. They walked back to where a young hobgoblin girl was crying.

Horra hurried out of the park, relief making her limbs lighter. She strode toward the edge of town. Pidge was finishing the bread when she found a spot in a hilly crevasse behind a copse of trees. The snow wasn't deep beneath the dirt shelf and it was hidden enough to remove her hood so they could eat.

The sausages needed to be cooked, so she grabbed a few dry limbs from a dead tree, and with a snap of her claws, started a small fire. Pidge uncharacteristically stayed close by as she gathered the sticks and huddled by the fire.

Horra speared a sausage on a limb and roasted it while she nibbled on the bread she had smeared lavishly with the cheese and pondered the wedding.

It was five days away. She had six or seven days before it was too late to replant the seed. And she had to replant the seed, or the Erlking wouldn't be stopped. Horra opted for the six-day window just to be sure. That wasn't much time considering she'd already spent half of the fortnight wandering around the Wilden Lands, lost and then stormbound.

Though she was close to Hobgoblin Pass, she didn't trust that she was free and clear even though she had the woodencloak protecting her. Nothing had gone her way so far. She sighed.

Her mission to save the seed was imperative. But her father and her kingdom had to be rescued.

It was an impossible situation.

If she went to the Weald, she wouldn't make it in time to keep her father from marrying the fairy queen. If she went to try to save her father, would she get the seed to the Weald in time?

The trees around her creaked. She glanced around, but the wind was minimal now. No animals in sight. Ignoring it, she ate. Unfortunately, she ate so quickly that her stomach ached.

Horra flicked the last bit of meat and cheese to Pidge. The

sun was moving from its highest position in the sky. It wouldn't take long before its warmth would be gone again and darkness would settle over the area. She drew circles in the snow.

One, she could go back to Nomans Castle and save her father. Now that she knew where she was, two days travel from the castle, she could make it there in time to unmesmerize her father, kick the glittering fairies out, and have enough time to get the seed planted.

Or two, go to the Weald, plant the seed, and head then back to Nomans. It was a two-day walk, a day's wagon ride, to the forest. Not enough time to get there and get back to the castle before the wedding, though.

"Ugh!" She dropped her head in her hands. The urge to throw up was getting stronger.

She leaned back on the tree to ease her discomfort.

"*I understand your quandary, Princess. You must get the seed to the Weald or no one will be able to stop the Erlking. There are spies everywhere trying to stop you. The odds are against you making it to the Weald, let alone to the castle and then to the Weald.*"

Tears pooled in her eyes. "But I can't abandon my father when he's obviously under the Erlking's spell. I can't let him marry that stupid fairy. My kingdom's existence depends on me saving him from this marriage."

"*I may not be able to help you if you head back to your kingdom. The closer you get to the Weald, the more help I can give you.*"

"You brought me the woodencloak. Can't you take the seed to the Weald?"

"*Only lifeless objects can be transported. The seed has life inside it. I cannot transport it.*"

"I left because I thought my father was probably dead. I

know the seed is important, really, I do. But I can't let my father or my kingdom down. I have to go back and save them."

The tree she leaned against popped and creaked against her. The silence weighed on her like a reprimand, which she'd had loads of experience with. Guilt niggled at her gut. No matter what issues she and Woodsly had with her behavior and rebellion at times, she knew he had her back and would never let her down. He hadn't in the last moments of his life. He'd thought of her and prepared her the best he could. She owed him.

Light from the sun brightened slightly as it lowered in the sky, closer to staring her in the face. Her father's image wavered in her mind, of him smiling at her mother and her when she was little. Of him, after her mother passed and the absolute devastation he tried to hide in his dark eyes. He'd become hard and aloof. Horra understood the need to put your heart behind a wall to keep it from being hurt again. She'd done it as well. "I have to save my father and my kingdom, Kryk. I give you my word if I fail to save them, I will get to the Weald as fast as I can."

"The survival of the Wilden Lands rests on your word, Princess. Time to prove who you are." Kryk's voice became thready, tired. But the sentiment hit home and the weight of his expectations dropped on her shoulders like a hammer on an anvil. It took all of her willpower not to slump.

Horra gathered Pidge in her hood again, her hold unsteady. The pudge wudgie was getting used to that mode of travel so she circled and settled down quicker than before. They headed back into the hamlet.

They made it across Bough Valley faster this time, with Horra more confident in the woodencloak's ability to hide her appearance. The sun was low in the sky when a wagon clinked and clanked behind her. She stood aside to let it pass, and recognized it as being one of the peddlers who sold items to her castle. Maybe he was headed to Nomans!

She jogged to catch up with it. The door on the back of the wagon rattled, ajar, so she grabbed for it. It swung open and she pulled, making it inside before a wheel *thunked* into a rutted hole and swung the door shut behind her.

Inside, the wagon was full of kitchen utensils, jars of liquids, and covered crocks. It smelled of dust, feet, and pungent cheeses. At the back of the wagon was a small, lumpy cot, which the peddler must use for sleeping. A small cage holding a rodent sat on a shelf above the bed. Horra wondered why a peddler would keep such a pet when the eyes glowed green and it hissed at her, thrashing in the metal container.

Horra's eyes widened. It must have mange, though no sores scarred the critter's emaciated body. It was disconcerting, so Horra moved as far away from it as possible. After a few moments, the creature dropped to the bottom, heaving, and staring at her.

She'd considered jumping back off, but she needed a faster way to get to the castle. She could get both of her missions done if she could just travel faster than she had been. Besides, since when did a rat scare her? She'd stay only until the cart slowed and then she'd get off.

That decided, Horra leaned against the only free spot, the door, and stuck the knapsack behind her head. Chilled, she took the cloak off, and sticking her arms through the sleeves, put it on backward so it covered her cold front side. She snuggled down, ignoring the faint squeaks that came from the cage.

Freed, Pidge fluttered around, gobbling up whatever crumbs she could find. A smart bird, she stayed well away from the cage, which told Horra there was definitely something wrong with the vermin.

She planned what she'd do once she got to the castle. First, she'd find her father. She'd use the counter-spell in the Medicinal Curse Book to un-mesmerize him. She recognized all of the ingredients. It was just a matter of gathering them, putting them together, and getting the person to ingest the antidote.

Maybe then she'd un-mesmerize the fairies, too, so they would go back to their kingdom. And stay there forever.

After that, she and her father would head to the Weald to plant the seed. Satisfied with her plan of action, at least on the whole, she closed her eyes and let the swaying motion lull her into a deep sleep.

Horra woke when the door behind her opened. She landed in the snow, and her knapsack and cloak fell to the side of the road near the trees.

She wasn't sure who was more surprised—her for having landed in the cold snow or the hobgoblin who opened the door. Quickly though, the hobgoblin's eyes glazed over, and he stiffened.

Pidge darted out of the cart above her. Horra flipped over to get up but was halted when the hobgoblin grabbed her by her collar. He yanked her back and threw her into the cart.

Startled by the hobgoblin's strength, she kicked, but her boot made contact with the door. Something clunked against the wood, like a chain. A resounding click confirmed her fear.

She was locked inside.

"No, no, no!" she cried out, but it was no good. The cart began moving.

CHAPTER 24

Horra pounded on the door with her fists until they ached. She shivered. The snow had soaked through her clothes, and wearing no cloak, she was chilled. And scared.

Vinegar and beans! There were no windows in the wagon. She tapped on the floorboards of the cart, hoping one of them might be loose. The cart, however, was sturdy. Not even a board creaked. The cart jostled back and forth, almost as if moving quickly, quicker than normal. It made searching nearly impossible since she was jounced about like she was being shaken in a jar. She tried with no luck.

The wagon lurched and stilled. Her stomach churned. Where were they?

She grabbed a frying pan and readied to swing it. She could hear talking, but they were speaking low enough that she couldn't tell what they were saying.

The pan was heavy. Her arms soon ached, but no one came.

She lowered the pan. Were they going to leave her there? The chains clanked and the door jerked open.

Twilight greeted her along with the hooded Erlking, a pan flute in his hand. Accompanying him was one of their muscle-bound door trolls, whose eyes were quite blank and unemotional. Along with them stood the two worqs from earlier that morning. The hobgoblin peddler was nowhere to be seen, but sweetsuckle lingered in the air and a cold chill from a glowing path on the ground gave her goosebumps. *Fairies!* No wonder they got here so fast.

But if the worqs were here, where was Torren?

She held the pan up and tried to look as menacing as she could. They faced her castle's stables. Muted whinnies and sounds of work in the buildings carried on the breeze along with the scent of manure.

"Welcome home, Princess."

The Erlking was eye to eye with her, though she stood in the cart and he on the ground. Up close, his skin was eerily translucent and his smirking lips pale but dark at the corners. His eyes were solid black with no whites, shadowed, and sunken like he was a living, breathing corpse. The black cape hung on his skeletal frame.

Nervous, she said the first thing that came to mind. "A few root vegetables, maybe a good porcupine stew, would put some meat on those bones of yours."

The Erlking ignored her comment though she thought it was quite helpful. "You've arrived just in time for the nuptials. Just as I had planned."

What did he mean she arrived just as he planned? "Where's my father?" she demanded. Kryk's comments about her being watched returned. She fought to hold the heavy pan steady though her hands shook.

"I assure you he's safe." The Erlking pointed a bony finger at the two worqs. "Please assist the princess down."

The bigger worq grunted and lifted a hand to her. She swung the pan and caught the tips of his fingers. He jumped back. A snarl lit up his too-round face. He reached out as if to slap her, but the Erlking stopped him with the fairy queen's scepter. The globe of pearl was no longer white but a dingy gray. Sparks like lightning buzzed around the jewel.

An evil smirk stretched across his pale face. "I thought your old instructor taught you some manners. Not much of a tutor, was he?"

Her stomach roiled and burned. "Woodsly had more etiquette and breeding in his tail than you will ever have."

The figure's sallow face darkened. "Yes, well, at least I'm still here, aren't I?"

Her cheeks heated and her grip tightened on the pan's handle.

"Grab her, and don't be gentle." He nodded his head at the others and walked away.

The worqs and the troll jumped at her, and she swung the pan. She hit the troll on his head, hoping it might knock some sense back into his traitorous head. But, before she could swing the pan again, the worqs had her by the arms. They yanked her from the wagon, each pulling hard in different directions.

Her shoulder socket popped, and she hit the ground on her left side, bruising her hip. Alarm reeled through her when she remembered she didn't have the seed. She'd put it in the knapsack after speaking with Kryk. The sack had fallen out of the wagon with the woodencloak on top when the hobgoblin kidnapped her.

With renewed panic, she kicked and clawed, managing to get in a couple of good hits. The smaller worq landed a strike against her cheek, splitting her lip. Pinpoints of light dotted her sight. He might not have been good at playing the pan flute, but he was good at hitting.

Horra swung, kicked, and wiggled, getting loose a couple of times, but it was no use. The three of them were too big and strong for her to overpower, and she could no longer see out of her swollen right eye.

The larger worq tossed her down, and her face smashed against the ground. She sucked in air, but it was agonizing. Her lip swelled like her eye. The worqs jerked her up, and pain burst anew. She coughed and then groaned.

They dug into her pockets but found nothing. Nothing because everything she owned had gotten left behind, including Pidge.

They dragged her by the arms, each step painful. They entered the castle. She tried to lift her head to see where they were going, but one of them pushed it down, so she stopped trying. Luckily, she knew the castle enough to realize where they were headed, and her blood chilled. This was the way to the dungeon.

The hallway had steps down to the underground, where barred rooms were dimly lit with torchlight. Mice scurried around, and Horra remembered them swaying to music when she escaped the hooded figure before. Having seen the door troll under the Erlking's control was disheartening. Obviously strong in body did not equal strong in mind. Was she the only one who wasn't affected by him? How could that be?

They traveled past several occupied cells, all ones she had played in as a child at one time or another. Her pants tore on the cement flooring and scraped at the hide on her knees. Pain and exhaustion weighed her down and she slumped deeper and deeper in agony.

Though she could tell the cells held prisoners, she couldn't tell who they were. Dissenters, since they'd had no prisoners before the Erlking had come. But who were they?

Finally, they arrived at one of the last cells beside the sewer chute. It was smaller, damper, and darker than the others. Water dripped and sewage scents coated the air. One of the worqs opened the barred door and threw her in.

"Misbehave and we'll send you down the chute," one worq growled. The other laughed as they left.

Pain wracked Horra from her injuries and her heart. The tears she held back before now overwhelmed her, and she sobbed into the gritty floor.

"Who's there?"

The voice was familiar but raw and gravelly, so she couldn't place it.

She didn't answer.

"Don't worry. I can't hurt you." Heavy chains clanked. "I'm a prisoner, too."

"Who are you?" The question was weak, less than a whisper.

"Name's Balk. Who're you?"

CHAPTER 25

It was the bocan! "How'd you get here? I believed I'd lost you on the road to Hobgoblin Pass." Her voice cracked.

"Princess?"

She lay gingerly on her side. "Yeah."

"Sorry about that, Princess. They hijacked me and took my wagon, the thieves. Then after they used my face for jousting practice, they threw me in here. I wouldn't give your dungeon high ranks, though. No room service." He chuckled. "There's plenty of rats, though, if you like that kind of thing."

She grimaced. Mice counted as Pidge treats, not a meal. "I don't."

"You might if you get hungry enough."

She doubted it, but knew she'd do anything to survive. She didn't want to think about that right now, though. Not with her stomach tied in knots as it was.

The dungeon looked different now than when she was a child playing in the empty cells. Then it had been an adventure. And they rarely had any prisoners, at least not since the War of the Warts.

Each cell was encased in two-stone thick walls with hefty chains hammered into the back wall, except for this last one she occupied. This cell was cruder—almost as if finishing it had been an oversight by her foremothers. The cells were staggered so prisoners couldn't see into the ones on the opposite side.

"We're not alone?" she asked, knowing the answer.

"No. There were some thrown down here when they didn't cooperate with the Erlking. Dignitaries, by the insults the guards used when they arrived. Others were sent away."

Fear settled like a heavy ball in the center of her chest. Sent where? "My father?" She turned her fat lip to the cold floor. Maybe it would ease the swelling.

Balk grunted. "Somewhere drugged up in the castle, if you believe worqs' gossip."

She remembered her mother telling her about a secret tunnel in the dungeon. However, she'd never found it. She'd only been brave enough at the time to look in the first cells, and then she'd found the pudge wudgie egg and spent most of her time in the Conservatory.

She wished now she had taken more time to explore the dungeon. "We need to find a way out of here." The damp cold of the cell, and being dragged through the snow, made her shiver.

"If you have any tips on how to do that, Princess, count me in. I'll even give up my claim to the dagger."

Horra would've laughed, but it hurt too much. "It returned to me the moment they hijacked you and you couldn't live up to your end of the bargain."

He chuckled. "Ah, yes. Sorry. I had intended to fulfill that oath."

She worked her way up to sitting against the cement block wall. "Can't be helped, I suppose."

"How'd you get out of that one? I don't have a trapdoor for

the holding box, and they told me they knew you were on board."

Would it be in her best interest to tell him she had the candy and the cookie? Probably not since she didn't have her knapsack now, anyway. Not that they would've allowed her to have it when they threw her in here. It may have been a good thing they left it behind. Thankfully, Pidge was alive and small enough now she wouldn't be easily spotted. But her heart ached for her missing pet.

Her body was heavy. She couldn't find the energy to move. "I'm tired. I think I'm going to rest now."

"Beat you up a bit, too, eh? We can talk later, Princess. We have all the time in the world, or at least until starvation or the crud takes hold."

She frowned at his words and prayed it wouldn't be the latter.

Horra slept fitfully. When she woke, she was clammy with chills and had a headache. She never had headaches. A groan slipped past her lips.

"You okay, Princess?" Balk sounded as if he had just woken up as well.

"Dandy. Is it time for high tea?"

That drew a chuckle from the bocan. "You just missed it. It was delicious."

Horra stretched and groaned when her injuries protested. Every part of her body ached. She still had trouble seeing out of her swollen eye, and the cut on her lip split back open and stung when she talked.

"Yeah, that first time waking up and remembering what happened is always the best." His chains clanked as he moved.

"I wonder why they didn't chain me up like they did you."

"Probably because I come from a long line of swordsmiths,

though I rejected that lifestyle for the life of a mercenary." He chuckled.

"So, what you're saying is you can manipulate metal. That's why you coveted my dagger so much. But, why can't you get out of the chains, then?" Horra asked.

He grunted. "Enchanted. I can't break them. Do you still have that dagger?" Longing filled his tired voice.

That made her curious. "Enchanted? Our chains have never been enchanted. Hold on, you rejected being a metalsmith or you were stripped of the title? How do they know about you, then?"

Several moments passed before he responded. "You're too smart for your own good, you know that? The Erlking has spies everywhere."

"I've done a lot of extra homework. I know enough about goblin society to know you'd be an outcast, shunned." None of his kind would come to his aid. No wonder he couldn't get details about his daughter's death. None of his kind would be required to tell him anything.

She shifted when her leg cramped. "Wish I did have the dagger, though. I would've done a lot more damage if I had."

His chains clanked as he moved around. "You probably wouldn't have been spared if you had. These guys aren't exactly playing around."

She rubbed her sore lip. "So I noticed."

"I don't suppose you have any allies that haven't been mesmerized?"

"I wish I knew. There was a deaf kitchen hobgoblin who came to my rescue. She smacked the Erlking with a pan, and that's how I got away from him the first time. I don't know her name, though. And if any of the royal female trolls remained free, we should've seen them by now. They're oathbound to take up arms to defend our kingdom."

Scratching, squeaking noises like mice running across the floor echoed.

Thump.

"Ah, dinner is served." Balk's chains rattled.

Her queasy stomach flipped over. It was one thing for Pidge to do it. It was quite another to think of a higher being eating a raw rat. She clutched her stomach and breathed shallow breaths so she wouldn't throw up.

Chains from a different part of the dungeon clanked.

"Who's that?" she asked Balk.

"One of your royal female trolls, I believe. Possibly an ambassador if I heard the guards correctly." He sounded as if he were chewing.

Horra gagged and bile burned her throat. Her mind went back to the grand dinners she'd had so many times before without a care for how the food got there. Porcubeasts with their spikes served crunchy sides up. Or pickled parsnips with devil's root jelly. She longed for it, could almost taste it. A deep breath of the dirty, musty cell broke the spell of her mind's wandering. It wasn't a good sign that her mind was playing tricks on her.

More rattling brought her back to what she'd been considering before her thoughts had followed the rabbit trail into food. Which of her ambassadors was locked up? The consequences were staggering.

What if there was no one to help her now? The seed wouldn't get to the Weald. The Erlking wouldn't be defeated. The Wilden Lands would fall.

She'd be the first defeated ruler of Oddar. Shame rocked her. She should've listened to Kryk. Who was she to make decisions for her kingdom when every time she did, it ended in getting lost or captured? Disappointment and disgrace lodged in her throat and she couldn't swallow it down.

"Your silence is deafening, Princess. A tin cent for your thoughts."

She disguised her sob as a cough. "They're not worth the fuzz in your pockets at the moment."

"Don't give up so easily. There's always hope until there's no hope. And I'm here to tell you we still have hope."

"How can you be so confident? You do realize I'm only thirteen and small for my age? I've been coddled most of my life. I have book knowledge, but little if any experience. I'm way over my pointy ears with this ... Erlking." She shifted, wishing for a blanket or anything soft to ward off the cell's unyielding chill. The darkness around her seeped inside her heart. "If you put your hope in something, I suggest it not be me."

"But you're a troll princess. And trolls are the fiercest warriors in all of the Wilden Lands."

She gave a bitter laugh. "I'm not a warrior if I die in this prison."

"You won't die here. I had a vision. It was of you standing over the Erlking with that jeweled dagger at his throat. I also saw my daughter again. So, you see? We're both going to make it out of this. My visions are never wrong."

"Since when do bocans become seers?" His daughter Floke was dead. He'd said so himself. He must be having hallucinations. Like hers with the food.

A door creaked and grit crunched under someone's shoes as they walked toward her. Horra shrank back when the worq who had dragged her into the dungeon appeared at the barred door. He had manacles in his hands.

"Did you get a good night's sleep, Princess?"

She refused to answer, and he laughed and unlocked her cell. "Time to go visit your new step-mommy."

CHAPTER 26

Horra crawled away from the worq. He followed her around the back of the cell until he had her cornered. He clapped the manacles on her wrists and pulled her out of the cell by the chains.

He looked over and snorted at Balk in the cell beside hers.

Horra tripped and fell over the metal door frame. The worq yanked on the chain and enjoyed watching her struggle as her legs wobbled. Her whole body ached but now her arms burned as well.

She was almost positive she spied a female troll in one cell. Their green hair was matted and they were curled up, whimpering in the corner.

Outside, the sunlight was bright. Though she'd never had trouble going from dark to light before, the light was painful to her eyes, well, eye. She could only see with one eye. The other was still too swollen.

He led her around to the front of the castle to the receiving room where all of the creatures always waited for an audience with the king. Surely, he wasn't going to drag her through the crowds to make a spectacle of her?

But that was obviously his intent.

The front room was full of creatures from across the Wilden Lands. There had to be almost a hundred or more. Shock silenced the crowd for a moment before noisy chatter exploded. There were no nods or thumping fists to chests. Instead, gnomes spewed insults, and imps spat on her. Redcappers laughed at her. There were even a few spriggans who joined the frenzied crowd. She recognized some of them from previous Goblin Courts, troublemakers who didn't like her father. Now that she was brought in on charges, they were overjoyed. Celebratory, even.

It probably didn't help that she looked like a criminal, all battered and bloody and being escorted in shackles.

The worq shoved through the center of the crowd and she was surrounded by a wall of clamoring creatures, all yelling or laughing at her. She couldn't avoid the grabs and things hurled at her. This never would happen if her father were in charge and in his right mind. If nothing else, he had dignity and honor for himself, other creatures, and their kingdom. She didn't have time to contemplate what it all meant.

They reached the granite doorway into the throne room, and her captor lifted the huge brass knockers. She'd always hated the sound of the door knocker, which meant she was going to have a late Goblin Court day. But it would never equal how much she hated the sound now that she was on the other side of the door.

The doors were opened by the traitorous door troll. Again, he was unemotional, disconnected. Just doing a job he's done enough he could do it in his sleep. Possibly, it's what he thought he was doing right now.

More people lined the throne room on either side of a light

blue carpeted runner that led to the stone thrones. Or at least it used to lead to the granite and marble thrones. They were gone. In their place were two carved, tree-like seats with flowery cushions.

Queen Stella Toppenbottom sat on the more feminine carved chair. The other chair was empty.

Fury dimmed Horra's minimized eyesight for a moment. She unconsciously clenched her hands, but the manacles cut into her wrists. She swallowed back the pure rage at the glittery trespasser sitting pretty as you please. As if she belonged there.

"Darling. I see the news that they found you is true." The queen lofted a glance at the worq. "What are her charges?"

"What? What are you doing?" Horra narrowed her eye. Did the queen think she could hold court in *her* kingdom?

Stella perused a scroll given to her by the worq and then handed it to a herald. The queen tittered. "Why, I'm charging you, of course. You have a glut of charges."

Horra glanced around the room, waiting for someone to stand up for her or take her side. No one did. She noted all who were present. "You're not a troll. You can't hold court. Where's my father?"

"He's recuperating from the injuries you gave him before you attacked my daughters and stole that priceless animal."

"I never hurt my father or your daughters. The last time I saw my father, he was with you! If anyone here is to blame for harm done him, it would be *you!*"

"I thought you might try to get out of your charges. See, if you played nice, I would've let you go to the wedding. But it seems that that is not to be." She glanced over at the worq. "Her charges?" Her voice no longer held a chiming tone. It was distinctly nasty.

The worq smiled. "Conspiracy to kidnap, attack with bodily harm—several instances—theft of a priceless bird."

The Queen arched her brows. "How do you plead?"

The fairy sat there so regally as if she had always belonged there. Horra couldn't believe her eye. She was supposed to be the judge, not the judged.

Besides, none of the charges were true and no discussion was entered in to decide what had truly happened as was customary. This was nothing but a sham, though she didn't expect anything different. "Innocent."

Several gasps echoed through the chamber. Everyone present was surprised except the worq. A vicious smile slashed across his gruesome face.

The fairy dipped her head in acknowledgment. "I remember your grandmother, Queen Petra, being just as stubborn as you when we fought the Erlking. She took risks which resulted in many of my army getting butchered."

Outrage jolted through Horra. She knew fairies lived a long time but didn't realize the current queen had been seated that long. Fairies weren't something she liked to study, so she avoided them. Even if the fairy queen hadn't been mesmerized, she could easily take her revenge on Horra for what she perceived as her grandmother's sins.

The queen gave her a slight smile. "Your punishment will be twenty-five years in the dungeon, starting today. Take her away."

Horra tugged at the manacles, wishing she could use them to squeeze the last glittering, glowing inch of life from the queen's body. Mesmerized or not, the queen would pay for her deceit.

The worq yanked on Horra's chain and sharp jabs of pain reminded her she was in no shape to try to fight back. She stumbled out of the throne room and back into the waiting room where they kicked and spat on her some more before she made it through to the outside again.

Horra was dragged past the kitchen, where the door opened and a hobgoblin limped out. She managed a glance and recognized the servant who had aided her when she ran from the Erlking the night her father disappeared. Before Horra could manage to say anything, the worq yanked her past. Her shoulder popped and Horra squealed.

They were at the steps to the dungeon in seconds. The worq rushed down the stairs, and she failed to keep up with him. She fell on the last stair and landed hard on the dungeon's stone floor.

She refused to get back up. The worq was going to have to drag her this time. It had to be harder on him than jerking the chain around when she participated. It was a small satisfaction, though the worq only laughed and left whistling a merry tune.

Her sole saving grace had been the vapid vestra jacket, which kept her from scraping against the floor. Her red hair, however, was snarled and stuck out wilder than ever before.

"Princess?"

Her breathing was labored due to the pain still radiating from bruises and injuries all over her body. She lay sprawled on the cold floor, glad for the numbing chill this time. "Mmmmhmmm."

"You have two choices as I see it. Give in and let them win ... and die without fulfilling your destiny. Or get mad as a bungbee and find a way to sting them back."

CHAPTER 27

Horra drifted in and out of sleep, waking only to pain and cold. Dark shapes with glowing eyes and chiming voices chased her through thorn-filled forests. Poisonous air choked her, but she was unable to get away.

A cool hand drifted across her forehead.

"Mama?" Horra called out. Maybe if she died, she could join her mother and they'd be happy again.

Yes, that's what she wished.

"You must eat something, Princess Horra. You have to regain your strength."

Hot liquid filled her mouth, and Horra sputtered. She opened one eye—the other was covered with something cold and pasty—and the hobgoblin's bleary form came into her limited view. Horra was lying close to the barred side of the cell where the worq had left her and the servant was trying to feed her some type of broth.

"Good evening. It's not too hot, is it? I made sure to get it bubbling hot so it wouldn't grow cold before I got down here."

"Wha—" She touched the compress on her eye, but the hobgoblin slapped her hand away.

"Don't take the compress off. There's no time for questions. Just eat." She jerked a glanced back over her shoulder. "But do it quick-like. They could come at any time to check on you again." The old hobgoblin reached in, her gnarled hand holding a wooden spoon full of steaming soup.

"You can hear?" Horra should've been offended, but she nodded and opened her mouth.

"Of course I can hear. Luckily for you, too. I take my hearing aid out when I go back upstairs so I'm not affected like the others." She spooned more broth into Horra's mouth.

It was the best thing she'd tasted in a while. She swallowed, coughing as it caught and burned down her parched throat. The hobgoblin wiped her face and continued to feed her. Horra did her best to eat, but she tired easily.

"Rest up. I'll be back soon." The hobgoblin servant got up and handed a cask of something to the bocan.

"Thank-ee."

"See that you hide that or we'll both be flayed. Remember our arrangements."

The bocan grunted in response.

Horra's eyes were heavy, as was her aching body. Had the hobgoblin drugged her? She couldn't stay awake and sank into a dark sleep.

The next thing she knew the worq was slapping her face. She rolled away from him, groaning when she put weight on her injured shoulder. Her tormentor chuckled before footsteps echoed away from her. Sleep called her back again.

"Princess Horra."

It was the hobgoblin servant.

"Mnnnya." Horra smacked her pasty lips to try to get them to work.

"Roll my way. I have more food for you, but I can't reach you."

It took effort to flip to her stomach and lift herself up to move. Faintness stole her eyesight for a moment, and she breathed deep to regain her wits. Slowly, Horra crawled over toward the bars.

"Got you some of your favorite bracken bread. Freshly baked with bacon grease on it."

Horra's mouth watered. She reached for it, but could only use her right arm, her left arm was still out of joint.

She took it from the servant. "Thank you." The first bite washed over her senses. Gooseflesh rippled across her hide, and she quivered. "Mmm." She shoved half of the piece into her mouth and leaned back against the bars as she savored it.

"That's it. Makes my heart glad to see you able to eat on your own, Princess." The hobgoblin gave her another slice dripping with grease. Next, she handed her a goblet full of sour spruce juice. "I added some coo-coo powder for the pain. It'll help you heal as well."

"How long was I asleep?" Horra took a giant gulp of the sour drink. It was refreshing. She finished the second slice of bread and the juice. "Thank you again—" She hesitated. "I don't know your name."

"Sageel, mistress. And you've been out the better of two days. Count yourself among the lucky ones. Many of your warriors fell when the worqs arrived." The hobgoblin refilled the goblet gave Horra a hunk of meat. "This is cold, and I dug it out of the trash, but it's still good. Those no-good fairies don't eat anything but insist upon a full table. Such a waste!"

So, her warriors had come to the rescue only to be overpowered. That was not good news. She did the math in her head. It had been nine days since she fled the castle. Or was it ten? She'd lost count, and time, like her energy, was running out. "How did you escape after you hit the Erlking?"

Sageel cackled. "I'm a good actress. He doesn't know I'm not under his spell." She prodded Horra's eye, which though still swollen, she could see out of once again, and glanced over her shoulder. "I must go, though, or someone will suspect something. Eat that meat. I'll be back soon."

"But—"

Before Horra could finish the sentence, Sageel was gone.

She picked at the meat. It was a bird of some kind, with a fruity aftertaste. Horra frowned but wasn't going to complain about finally having food again.

"You doing okay?" the bocan called out to her.

"Better. You?"

"Great since your favorite maidservant found you here." He burped. "Not bad if you're into exotic birds."

An image of Pidge flashed through Horra's mind. She stopped chewing and glanced at the meat. Her stomach twisted. What if ... but it couldn't be, could it? Her stomach bulged. It had shrunk from not eating. She would save the meat for later.

"We need to convince Sageel to try to find the keys so we can get out of here."

Horra agreed. "What was that she said about an arrangement?"

Balk groaned. "No one trusts a bocan. I had to make an oath for her to feed me. When, or if, I get out of here, I'm obliged to return her to her home in the half-lands."

"Sounds like a pretty good deal for her."

He grunted. "Ever since that bird snuck in here, there haven't been any mice. I had to eat something."

Horra's ear twitched. "Bird? What bird?"

"Black bird. A real hunter, that one." He laughed. "It visited your cell a few times, making a big fuss of noise."

Horra sat up so fast that her body screamed in pain. "Pidge?" She whistled.

A screech answered her. A shadow flew through the bars, and Pidge landed on her lap.

CHAPTER 28

"Oh, Pidge! I didn't think I'd ever see you again!" Horra gathered the bird close and rubbed her face in the softness beneath its chin.

Pidge fluffed her feathers and screeched.

"She's yours?" Balk's voice was a grunt mixed with a chuckle.

"Yes. I raised Pidge from an egg. And you said she?" Horra sat the bird on the floor.

"Clearly. The male pudge wudgies are the domesticated ones. They don't hunt near as well as the females. That bird there is a she."

Horra had never known for sure, had only assumed, and since they only had one there was no way to tell. "She's an excellent hunter. Huntress? Anyway, I'd starve before she would."

"That I can believe. So, do you think there's a way out other than the entrance if she found her way in?"

Horra petted Pidge on her head and fed her the last of the meat Sageel had given her. "I doubt it since she was with me when I got captured. I'm not sure how she ended up back here. Maybe she has a homing ability?" Even though Horra hadn't gotten her hopes up, it still twisted her gut to think of never getting out of the dungeon.

Balk was quiet for a long while. Meanwhile, Pidge scoured Horra's cell for possible prey. She flittered here and there. Horra smiled at her hunting pet, glad to have some glimmer of goodness to focus on instead of her own circumstances.

Pidge pecked at the wall. Dirt and pieces of rock fell to the ground. When the pudge wudgie gave up on the wall, she fluttered back down to the floor, but something glittering on the spot Pidge had just pecked.

She got to her knees. Still weak and aching, she wobbled over to the wall and wiped some of the grime off the glittering spot. An obsidian stone was set inside a slab of rock. Heart pounding, Horra scrubbed at the wall around the stone with her claw, digging and scraping away the years of dirt build-up.

Just as Horra was about to give up and chalk it up to coincidence, she found a dragon's eye gem, then a blackstar jewel, and finally an onyx. Though each stone was black, she knew the difference in each stone's color and hardness by memory. "Oh my goodness!" she whispered.

"What're you up to, Princess?"

"Nothing." She scraped at the jewel pad until the tips of her claw bled, but it was worth it. Sequence after sequence she pushed into the gems, sequences that she knew from other rooms and had used so many times they were memorized. However, none of them worked.

Horra clutched her stinging appendages to her chest, frustrated. She slipped down to sit on the floor. The entry door to the dungeon clanked. Her heart stopped beating for a moment. She grabbed the glass and whistled quietly, calling to Pidge.

The bird flew over and landed on her knee. Horra slid over to the corner and placed Pidge in the space behind her, sealing her and the juice in between her body and the wall.

The clanking of chains and something being dragged echoed down the dark hallway. She was tempted to try to go see what was happening but chided herself. She couldn't give them the chance to find Pidge.

A cell door creaked open, and someone grunted when they were thrown inside. A low sound. Possibly male. The door clanged shut. Steps sounded away from them and then the dungeon door closed.

Horra waited some time before she moved away and let Pidge back out.

"Hello?" Balk called.

There was no answer.

"You don't think that was Sageel, do you?" she asked Balk, praying that the servant was still safe.

"Too big. You're bigger'n that hobgoblin and you made less noise than this one. Besides, the sound of the grunt doesn't fit a hobgoblin."

Horra let Pidge out and sat thinking about the gems and the sequence. Each room was different. She went through the different rooms in her mind and each passage's sequence, trying to figure out if there was a clue in them.

Over and over, she repeated it all in her head. Eventually, she tired. Pidge took off after something Horra couldn't see. She closed her eyes and dozed.

A vision of her mother showing her the passageways drifted to her in a semi-dream.

Her mother waved an arm around the space. "Our foremothers were the kingdom's most stellar stonemasons and jewelers. They built their campsite from the center out, which is why this passage seems like a space you'd find in a village square. They dug out the stones, gems, and jewels, and used the money to build the castle over the passageway. None but the royal line knew about it."

A younger Horra looked into her mother's brown eyes. "But, momma, where were all the boy trolls?"

Her mother brushed a lock of Horra's hair behind her ear. "They lived in the swamps. Swamptrolls weren't interested in being civilized until we warrior women became powerful." She chuckled, a deep throaty laugh. "Trolls are quite competitive. It was a couple of years later, after our foremothers had built the castle fully, when the swamptrolls decided to see what we had accomplished. It was so grand, that they decided to challenge us for it. Well, you can imagine our great, great, great, great foremother's reaction, can't you?"

Horra giggled. "They took up the challenge and fought to the death, defeating the biggest swamptrolls."

"That's right! But the perception of the swamptrolls had been changed because of all that the warrior trolls had accomplished. They left their swamps behind for the mountains, becoming more and more civilized. Our first queen, Queen Calcy, needed an heir, so she put out a call for the mightiest male troll. There was a festival held where the Conservatory is now. Whoever won the great battle could ask Calcy to marry them. A minertroll named Spratic beat out over a hundred trolls and won the bid for Calcy's favor. They married in the great chapel, and the rest is history."

Horra studied her mother's gleaming red hair and rugged, warty hide. She was strong and beautiful, everything Horra wanted to grow up to be. "But I have to keep the passages a secret, right, momma?"

Horra's mother's face shone with pride as she smiled down at her. "It's the brightest gem in our crown, daughter. Our God created trolls with the ability to do and build, but only warrior *trolls believed in the Almighty. He blessed us for that, and we promised in blood oaths and with sacred vows we'd keep our line pure. We built a mighty kingdom, even defeating the elves to keep it. Because the male trolls doubted the God of all creatures, they are not allowed to step onto this sacred ground. Remember, the best things in life come from hard work and sweat."*

"That's our motto." Horra grinned.

"That's right! Our foremothers built our kingdom through blood, sweat, and hard work—the bounty of a kingdom. This passage is for royal female trolls only, a special gift to our kind. May it serve you as well as it served me during the war."

Horra woke with a start, she'd been snoring. For a moment she grieved the disappearance of her dream. Her other self had been so real. As had her mother.

A shadow loomed to her right, and Horra squealed. It was Pidge, but she'd grown back to her normal size. "How'd you do it, girl? I don't have the giant's food."

Pidge fluffed her feathers and nudged Horra's claw. She scratched the soft feathers beneath Pidge's beak. Did that mean she was going to return to her shorter self? "How am I going to keep you safe now, girl?"

She had to find a way out of this cell. Her mother's words twirled in her mind. Something niggled at her. Something her mother said was important, but she couldn't put a claw on what it was.

Then it hit her. The brightest gems! That was the answer to the sequence. Everything was built in the order of necessity and importance. And each of the important places had gems assigned to them. But if a royal was ever jailed by the enemy, there was only one code that would save them—five black gems in order of rarity, but backward. That was it!

Horra pulled herself back up and punched the sequence into the wall.

CHAPTER 29

The wall clicked, and dirt and rock rained down as the gears behind the wall moved into action.

"What's going on?" Balk's voice held a note of alarm.

A section of granite wall shifted back and moved to the side. It ground and screeched with disuse as it moved. "I found it! I found the way to get out of here."

Pidge tottered, claws scratching against the rocky floor, and darted through the doorway.

"Wait! What're you doing?" Balk called out.

The split in her lip stretched as she grinned and she stepped into the narrow walkway. Pidge scuttled down the narrow passage, just wide enough for her to fluff her feathers without touching the sides but not tall enough to fly.

Horra moved back into the cell. "Balk, I can't take you with me. I promise to come back and get you when I can." Using the last of the spruce juice, she made mud and slathered it over the gems in case they came and inspected the cell after she left. Her movements were slower than she liked, having only the use of one arm. But, they couldn't find the passageway, no matter what. She'd also hide the cup, just to be sure Sageel wouldn't be revealed.

His chains rattled. "How—never mind. When they find you've gone, they're going to be *very* curious."

Though Horra now knew the character of the bocan, it was frustrating at the moment of escape to need him to keep quiet. She finished piling on the mud, content it blended into the wall. "What do you suggest?"

"Funny you should ask. I've had lots of time to consider my options. I would require an oath from you that you would rescue me at your earliest convenience. And I would need some form of weaponry when I am freed."

Horra sighed. "I am no longer in the possession of the dagger if that's what you're asking for."

Balk chuckled. "Your kingdom supplied gems to all the Wilden Lands. I'm sure you have something that will fund me finding my daughter."

"There's no way to do a blood oath this time, bocan. And you know as well as I do that spoken oaths do not bind trolls." She had no interest in performing a vow with him. That was binding until death.

"Aye, I do. But the Creature God blessed this mountain and your kingdom. You are bound to that magic, correct? I request a challenge to become the new Queen's Champion."

Horra froze, claws clenched. She knew what he meant, understood the implications. Her father had become Queen's Champion after her mother died, allowing him to accede to the throne until she was of lawful ruling age. And troll law was backed by the magic held in the mountain by oath and vow, essentially binding them to the Creature God. "What do you mean by requesting such a thing?"

Balk grunted. "I studied law once. Your father is no longer

fit to wear a crown. The fairy queen hasn't been made troll queen yet. By process of elimination, that makes you Heir Apparent, Princess. Therefore, you can choose a new Champion until you are old enough to rule. I will agree to your terms, as long as they are reasonable. The title itself holds power that can stop both the fairy queen and the Erlking from stealing the throne from you and your father."

She chafed at thinking her father wasn't fit to be king any longer, but she knew Balk was right. Her father lost the ability to rule their kingdom when the Erlking seized control. And there wasn't anything Horra wouldn't do to keep her kingdom from being taken over. It fell to her as the princess to make things right, and keep her kingdom safe.

Though she had been lucky in her dealings with Balk, he was a bocan and less than trustworthy. A band squeezed across her chest.

Could she do this on her own? If not, would Balk find a way to take advantage of the title and power? Options spun through her mind.

"Well?"

She stood taller. "I have a bargain for you, bocan. I declare you Champion Bearer, which gives you a temporary title and power, but relinquishes the crown back to my father when he becomes fit once again to resume his duties, or to me when this mess is over. And you must swear fealty to me alone. Then I will help fund your mission to avenge your daughter. May it be so."

He grunted. "I never said anything about swearing fealty."

"True, but I don't fully trust you. Even though you've confided in me about your daughter, you've failed me once already. Then there's the slight issue of your addiction to metal objects, namely my mother's dagger. You don't honestly think I'd give over my kingdom that easily, do you? It's this or nothing." Horra glanced at the doorway. What kinds of trouble could Pidge be getting into?

Balk's chains rattled. "You drive a mean bargain."

"May it be so?"

He groaned, and his chains clanked again. "May it be so." When Balk finished speaking, the ground around them shifted.

Horra fell to the floor, her arms out to catch herself. Her injured shoulder popped again and pain bloomed once more. Horra bit her lip against the agony as Pidge squealed somewhere in the distance. She tentatively moved her arm, and though it hurt, she had a better range of movement back.

The ground stilled and so did Horra. Nomans had a new, temporary ruler. The magic of the troll kingdom wouldn't accept the queen or the Erlking now, no matter how many ceremonies they held.

All she could do was hope she made the right choice. She rubbed her throbbing shoulder, turned, and stepped through the stone doorway, tucking the juice cup in a corner. Horra pulled the lever and the stone slab creaked and ground shut. There was no bolt to lock it. She supposed no one saw the need to lock a dungeon door.

Trembling from anticipation, Horra moved to the left, following after Pidge.

Dust and rubble littered the passageway, and the air held a stale stillness. She wondered how long it had been since anyone had traveled this particular path. It didn't look like it had been used since being created. Her mother had never shown her this particular set of passages, though she'd mentioned them. She probably never envisioned Horra being thrown into the dungeon. Horra wouldn't have believed it had she not lived it.

Water dripped from a distance. The tunnel opened up and Horra was glad to see Pidge flying around chasing mice.

After several feet, she came to a tunnel too small to walk

through. The opening above the tunnel was too high for her to climb up. Besides, she spied spiderwebs in the corners thick enough to remind her of the underside of the giant's bed. She shivered. Hopefully, these were old webs. Since they were thick with dust and gray from age, it reassured her it was safe. However, she'd be alert just in case.

Crawling on her belly, she got stuck in the enclosed hole at her shoulders. She pushed and wiggled loose and tried again, this time with her uninjured arm stretched out in front of her. She slithered along, frowning at the grit that rubbed her from head to toe. She spat out the dirt that coated her lips as she panted to get through. With a final push, she slipped through to the other side.

She went to dust herself off and laughed. There was no need. Her clothes were tattered, bloody, and now grimy beyond imagination. Wouldn't the redcapper laundresses love that?

Horra glanced around, realized where she was, and grinned.

CHAPTER 30

Horra inhaled a deep breath and pulled the lever at
the top of the stairs. Her heart pounded hard when
it took a few seconds longer for the gears to shift
into motion and move. Muted light and scents of hay and
horse dung flooded over her. A distance away a horse whinnied,
but otherwise, it was quiet.

She lifted the door on the stable floor, entering it. Hay and
dust rained down from above. An excited Pidge took off and
fluttered around the wooden beams, scaring off a few birds
nesting in the rafters. She understood the other bird's dismay at
being assaulted by a giant pudge wudgie.

Saddles, bridles, blankets, buckets, and other items lined
the wooden enclosure. Dust-coated streams of light filtered in
from the windows.

She crept to the front looking for anything she could use as
a weapon. Though there was no movement, as a young troll
she'd found hobgoblin stable boys sleeping in the hay from time
to time. She hadn't visited the stables for quite a while, mainly

because it was too hard to visit her mother's riding companion, Nimble.

The slate-gray, winged gulgoyle, a beast with flesh as tough as stone and long, bony wings, shook its head up and down at her. Once feared and hunted to extinction, it was the last of its kind. Even her mother had never dared to verify its gender. Her father hadn't had the heart to sell it or get rid of it, so the gulgoyle had been put to pasture. It couldn't fly away since it had had its wings clipped before her mother rescued it from a cruel dwarf.

After her mother died, Nimble had shed its feathers and lost its fire. The troll physician said it was because of stress. Horra knew it was from a broken heart.

Horra petted the gulgoyle's head. "I miss her, too."

Nimble nipped at Horra's shirt and bellowed a low, guttural sound.

Horra grabbed a bag half-filled with oats. Though usually a carnivore, Nimble dove into the bag, almost biting Horra's claw off in its haste. "Has anyone been feeding you? Probably figured you weren't worth anything without your feathers and fire, huh?"

While the gulgoyle munched on the oats, Horra grabbed a pail from a clasp on a post to draw water. But the well was outside. She glanced through the window facing the next stable. She waited while a worq crossed from the grand stable to the castle.

Soon, they'd notice her absence. And with her being larger now, it would be harder to hide if she needed to. She'd have to move fast.

Horra sprinted to the well and tied the bucket to the hook and dropped it in. Her battered arms burned with the effort to pull it back up. She gulped her fill quickly before carrying it back to the barn. Water sloshed over the sides on the way back to the stall.

Nimble sucked in long drinks while Horra caught her breath. There hadn't been any sign of weapons to arm herself. Shouts broke out from outside of the other stables, and Horra raced to the back of the enclosure to hide. She slid into the hay stall, between two rows of bales. Hay poked her from every direction.

The door creaked open.

"She's got to be somewhere. She can't have gone far. Get the beasts saddled, we need to find her." It was one of the worqs.

"Y-yes sir," came a hobgoblin's reply.

"And you were told not to feed this beast." The bucket crashed. Nimble cried out in pain.

Horra hunched down in the bundles, her fists clenched and shaking. Anger and fear warred inside her. It used to be easier to hide. She never thought she'd wish to be smaller again or to have magic so she could fight back. One of these days, she would make the worqs pay for their cruelty.

Footsteps shuffled past her to the end stall. She waited while they hauled several items out of the stable, and then waited a bit longer to be sure they were gone.

Hay poked her hide as she wriggled out of the bales. It stuck out of her hair and scratched under her tunic. She immediately headed to check on Nimble.

The gulgoyle lay on the floor, its featherless wings slumped to the ground instead of being tucked along its spine. A red stripe welted along its hind where the worq had whipped it. It didn't move as Horra opened the door and sat down to pet it.

Pidge fluttered down beside the gulgoyle and pecked at the pieces of oats that had fallen to the floor. Nimble made a feeble squawk but otherwise didn't move.

"I'm so sorry, Nimble. I promise they'll pay for that."

The gulgoyle lifted its head and placed it on Horra's lap. Anger burned from the innermost part of her being. This madness had to end now.

Horra searched the stable, finding a small jar of ointment she used on the gulgoyle's wound. However, there wasn't even a hammer to use as a weapon. She sighed and slid down a wooden post to sit.

A cacophony of noises filtered in. Worqs yelling at hobgoblins. The pounding of beasts' hooves as they took off to search for her. Screams from hobgoblins as the worqs beat them for not moving fast enough.

She covered her eyes with her hands.

"Princess?"

Horra started and glanced around.

"Behind you."

She spun around and came face-to-face with Kryk, the rood, who stared at her from the post she leaned against.

"Oh, thank goodness it's you. How did you—"

"I am not limited to live trees, Princess. But time is running out. Both for your father and the seed."

She ducked her head. "I know. And I lost the woodencloak and my knapsack that has the seed in it. They've figured out I'm missing and I don't know what to do."

"Which is why I'm here." One of the boards on the fencing moved out like an arm. The woodencloak dangled from it. "I've brought you back your cloak. I suggest you don't lose it again, or it will return to the Weald for good."

She grabbed the cloak, slipped it on, and hugged it tight to her chest. Tears blurred her sight. "Thank you. I won't. I promise."

Pidge flew down and landed on the fence. She fluffed her feathers and screeched several times.

"Your bird wishes to tell you that she brought your knapsack before she snuck into the dungeon to find you. It's hidden outside the Conservatory's hole."

"You understand my pudge wudgie? How did she bring the sack?"

"Roods understand all languages. I believe she used some of the giant's food. She's a smart bird." Kryk nodded toward Pidge. "Show her the way, my friend, and be swift." He turned toward Horra. "You have until sunset tomorrow, the twelfth day, before you must leave to get the seed planted, even if you have not saved your kingdom. All will be lost if you cannot get to the Weald in time." His face faded until the nose disappeared in the grain of the board.

Horra stood and adjusted the woodencloak.

The stable door opened.

CHAPTER 31

orra quickly wrapped her arms around Pidge, praying the woodencloak worked as she remembered. She held her breath while Torren hurried toward the back and grabbed a blanket, saddle, and bridle. Up this close, she could see his eyes were glazed, and a bit too fixed. Maybe he was mesmerized like all the others. She drew her chin up. It still didn't explain how he could speak worqen.

When he left, Horra let go of Pidge, who flew up to the roof and stared down at her. She waited a few seconds and glanced outside.

Several trolls, including Torren, rode out on the royal beasts, half to the south and half going east. The north side of the castle dropped off into cliffs, where she and Pidge had landed when they escaped, and the west was sloped down to the swamps. It served them right that they wouldn't find her. It gave her a great opportunity to snoop around.

Horra opened the stable door and let Pidge out. It was a short distance from the stables to the castle. Horra stopped when a maid hobgoblin came out of the castle to dump soapy water on the ground.

"Sageel!" Horra hissed out.

The hobgoblin glanced around, puzzled.

She reached out and touched the woman's arm. "It's me, Horra."

Sageel jumped. "Oh, my dear Princess." She narrowed her eyes. "Did they petrify you? Let me—"

"No. This is good magic but a long story."

The servant huffed out a relieved breath, one crooked hand clutched against her chest. "Well, you've got them quite disturbed, Princess. How did you escape the dungeon?" She shook her head. "Never mind. I don't want to know. You must hurry. Your father is set to be married tomorrow." Her face twisted. "To that glittery queen! You have to save us."

"I'm trying. I have a plan. First, I have to find my knapsack. Then I have to get into the lab to make an antidote to the Erlking's spell."

"Ah, yes! I knew you'd come through." Sageel clapped her hands. "But I must warn you, the Erlking has used much of our storehouses, and they're planning to destroy the gardens."

Horra's hopes crashed. "Woodsly used to have a stock hidden in his quarters. I'll try to find it if I need to." She squeezed Sageel's arm. "If you have a chance, can you keep an eye on Nimble? They've been starving the poor beast. Oh, and by the way, Balk is now my proxy."

The hobgoblin's bushy eyebrows rose, but she didn't question Horra. She nodded her head in agreement. "Be careful. They have traps set everywhere."

The Conservatory's hole was on the opposite side of the castle, and though disguised, she might attract attention, so she crept along the castle wall until the terrain became too rocky and steep. Loose, stony ground dropped off into craggy canyons, one of which she and Pidge had plunged down when they escaped from the Erlking days before.

Pidge flew ahead of her and circled back. Horra had always known her pet was astute for a bird. Now she wondered exactly what Pidge did know and understand.

Horra had always been agile climbing the mountain, but now that she'd grown some, she hoped it would be even easier. But she was bruised and battered, and scaling her way across the backside of the mountain castle was more difficult than she hoped.

Her boot slipped and she tumbled down, catching a limb before dropping too far. Her claws were raw and stung from digging out the stones on the dungeon wall. She reached for another hold, but her side cramped and her shoulder ached something fierce. Sweat dotted her brow and she took shallow breaths through the burning pain. She grasped a closer spot and pulled herself up carefully, step by step, until she crawled over the ledge.

Bright colors from the setting sun shone on the wall, casting the gray castle in a peachy-pink glow. It was a beautiful sight, calm and peaceful, so unlike what was truly happening. Melancholy hit her as she recalled how she had taken this for granted so many times. She never would again.

The hole wasn't far now, about the length of the throne room away, so she braced herself and kept moving closer.

She ignored the voice inside her head reminding her that night was falling on her eleventh day. Three days left to save the kingdom and get to the Weald.

Hoofbeats of the beasts returning from their unsuccessful search for her thundered from the other side of the castle. They weren't trying too hard to find her. She smiled to herself and kept moving.

The air grew colder as the sun dipped down. Pidge

screeched above her. The hole in the fence was still there. Either they weren't smart enough to cover it up, or it was a trap for her to come back into the castle. But the metal fence gaped open like always.

She whistled for Pidge. "Where's the knapsack, girl?"

The pudge wudgie swooped down into a thicket and screeched.

Horra hurried over to the weedy bush area and dug around. Her boot caught on something. As she moved to pull it out, she realized she'd stepped into a strap. She laughed, her relief mixing with elation. It was the knapsack.

She shuffled through the pockets to find everything she needed: The Medicinal Curse Book, the seed, the dagger, her compass, and the bag with the cookie crumbs and the candy. All there. Horra caressed the spotted seed, kissed the book, and flipped to the page which held the antidote to the mesmerization spell. She read through the ingredients and repeated them to herself several times in case she lost the book again.

Horra crawled back to the broken fence. To be sure it wasn't booby-trapped, she stuck a long stick through the hole and swung it around. It made contact with something hard. She bent to look through the hole but didn't see anything except the bark of the twisted tree. Another swing had no results.

No explosions, no piskies shooting off light in every direction. Nothing happened. A bulrahg croaked in the distance from the swamp. Pidge landed next to Horra and tottered through the opening.

"Wait, girl!" But, the pudge wudgie was too quick. Wood groaned and cracked as it shifted, moving out of the way for the bird. Pidge screeched in glee. Trees didn't just move—it had to be the roods helping them.

Horra reluctantly pulled the fence apart and stepped through the hole, careful not to snag the knapsack.

The Conservatory darkened as the sun sank. Ropy limbs from the tree Horra had used to lasso Pidge swayed. She laid a hand of thanks on the trunk.

"You're welcome, Highness," the tree spoke in her mind.

She patted the trunk and moved across the gardens in the direction of the lab and the secret passage doorway.

She was past halfway across the massive room when the two glass doors swung wide open. Tinkling voices broke the silence.

Piskies lit up the air as the two fairy princesses glided in.

CHAPTER 32

Horra dropped down between a brindle brush and some porcuvine bushes. She could spy on the frothy-dress-wearing fairies through the leaves. The piskies, with their shining wings, were inordinately energetic, flitting here and there in no apparent pattern, almost as if they'd imbibed on silly weed.

"Rot and ruin. Decay and disintegrate. Do your job. Wither and waste." The brunette dripped a few drops of something on the thorny henbane by the doorway. It shriveled and turned black instantly. They giggled and moved on to the poison persimmon, which was in full bloom.

The blonde repeated the brunette's words and dribbled the liquid onto the persimmon plant. It withered, the red blooms turning a sickly brown color. The fairies laughed some more and continued with their work.

Horra clenched her jaw and her tusks poked her lips. It was horrifying to watch the fairies kill her beloved plants so arbitrarily. No, she reminded herself. It was the Erlking's fault. As much as she wanted to hate them, the pink princesses were mesmerized. But she needed to get out before they found her. She slinked the remaining distance on her hands and knees toward the secret panel behind the curtain of vines.

Pidge fluttered to the ground and crawled through the vines with no trouble. She fluffed her feathers and gazed up at Horra, who was currently stuck in the barbs. She'd had no trouble when she was smaller getting through. A few minutes of maneuvering, however, and she managed to get free with only a couple of scratches.

"Good girl," Horra whispered and punched the jewels.

The door slid open silently. Without looking back, she slipped into the passageway, Pidge following her.

Once the panel shifted closed, Horra locked it and sat down on the gritty floor with her hands clenched in her hair. All of the plants in the Conservatory were being ruined. The urge to sit in a pool of her own pity flooded her. Woodsly hated self-pity. He always had something frustratingly helpful to say when she got all mopey. She took a deep breath and ran a grubby sleeve under her leaking nose. "I have too much to do. We have to hurry, Pidge. Or we won't save my father or my kingdom."

Pidge screeched in agreement and took flight. Horra hurried down the hallway to the lab and removed the bolt from the lock. Ear to the panel to check for sound, she tugged on the lever, and the wall shifted and opened to a dark room.

Shelves that had held jars full of ingredients in meticulous order had been rifled through and broken. Many of the jars were empty and some were smashed into pieces. Rows of planters were barren. Cupboards, which should've been locked, hung open, their contents missing. The doors had been broken and lay among the massive amount of debris left in their destructive wake. Few things remained untouched.

A frown pulled at her lips. How in the world was she

supposed to get the ingredients she needed and create an intricate potion in a short period of time if everything was wrecked? After searching for several minutes, she found a casting bowl and a broken alderwood spatula among the debris strung across the floor. She'd have to raid Woodsly's hidden cache of supplies for the rest of what she needed

She whistled to Pidge, who was busy nibbling at something crawling on a cluttered counter. The bird followed, a wiggling insect dangling from her beak.

Horra set the bar across the lock again and headed toward the bedchambers. Woodsly's quarters were situated between Horra's room and the king's suite. There wasn't a secret passage to it, but Horra could get there from her room or her father's suite if they weren't occupied.

The passage was comfortingly devoid of movement and sound. Horra fought off longing for the days when the worse thing she dealt with was hiding from the staff. She walked past her panel to the hole in the wall by the fireplace and gazed into her room. Bright, flowery chintz covered every inch of the room except the bejeweled walls, which were painted bright green. Her lumpy bed had been replaced by one with poles and wispy curtains. It was as if a fairy garden came and threw up in her room.

Gah! Where'd all of my stuff go?

She followed the dusty hall down past the instructor's quarters and arrived at her father's panel. Out of respect for her father, she hadn't used it since her mother died.

Memories of meeting her mother at this panel flew through her mind. Her heart clenched. She listened carefully for noises.

It was silent.

The stone panel ground as it opened due to disuse. Horra stood for a few seconds before peeking into the narrow opening, careful not to step into the room for fear of tripping a spell.

Like her room, a bouquet of flowers seemed to have exploded everywhere. Heeled shoes and dresses in exotic fabrics spilled out of the closet. This bed was frippery as well, only larger, with a puffy, cloudlike blanket on top. There was no sign of her father's possessions or what he had saved of her mother's things. Also missing was the case that held her mother and father's crowns. Her claws itched to burn it all down.

But that would draw attention to her, and she had bigger things than fairy fashion to take care of. She grabbed a flowery wicker ball from a stand next to the panel and rolled it across the floor to check for traps. It rolled across the room and down the stairs to the sitting area. Nothing happened.

She tiptoed across the bedroom to the stairs. The sitting area had several chaises and wicker furniture instead of the stone furniture her parents favored. Motion from one side of the area startled her and she let out a small gasp, and then laughed. It wasn't another person or a trap, but a large mirror. The frame was inset with pearls, shells, and coral, no doubt from the Great Sea which bordered the Fairy Overkingdom.

Horra turned in a circle to examine herself. "I look like a banshee." Her red hair frizzed out from her head in wild disarray, hay poking out in places. Cobwebs and dust covered her clothes, which were tattered and stained with dirt and blood. Her legs were longer, not quite as long as they had been when she'd climbed down the mountainside, but much longer than before she'd left.

She rubbed her fangs, which were growing into her adult tusks. They usually didn't set in until a troll turned fifteen. Maybe it had something to do with growing and shrinking and growing again? She'd have to do some research on the giant's concoctions after this was over.

Glancing back around, the urge to rub the muck and mire off with all the gauzy, flowered fabric almost overwhelmed her. She spat on the ground instead.

She never thought there was a green color she wouldn't like. She was wrong. The granite walls were covered in lurid green, like a real shade but with fairy dust and pixie wings sprinkled in. It was a glittery nightmare.

Knickknacks replaced the clay vases she'd made in art class and had given to her parents every year. It was all fragile and delicate, nothing that could've been created by hand. Temporary spells, she recalled from her lessons. Magicked into creation and short-lived. And it was as temporary as their stay in Nomans Castle.

Horra thumped a fist to her chest and clicked her tongue. "Hard work is the bounty of a kingdom." Her eyes welled. She closed them tight and sniffed, determining to make sure the fairies paid for their transgressions.

At the door, Horra stopped once again to listen for movement but it was quiet. She inched the door open and peered out into the hallway. Again, there was no movement or sound.

She left the door ajar and snuck down the hallway to the advisor's quarters and carefully entered, shutting the door behind her. Like the other rooms, the quarters were changed into a fairy wonderland. Pink colored the wall where Woodsly's herbal storage shelves were hidden. But this wall held no gems, nothing to punch in a code.

"How do I open it?" she whispered into the eerily fluffy room. She continued to run her claw across the stone but found nothing that triggered anything. In her haste to move over to the fireplace for a better look, she tripped over a fuzzy pillow on the floor and fell, face forward, to the ground.

Her claws stung from the impact. Her shoulder, though

back in place now, wrenched and throbbed. She kicked at the offending item on the floor and missed, hitting a wicker chair instead. Horra grinned. It only took a couple of good smacks on the floor to dismantle the chair. She tossed it into the fireplace and snapped her sore claws.

The wicker caught fire and glowing light flickered around the room, allowing her to see the wall better. But upon closer inspection, she found nothing that indicated a trigger switch. Tired and frustrated, she plopped down beside the fire to warm up and stared into the flames.

Ashes dropped from the wicker onto the formerly pristine hearth. Woodsly had been deathly afraid of fire, and, to her knowledge, he'd never lit one in this fireplace. It was always clean enough to eat on.

A silver hook on the side of the fireplace caught her eye. Horra slapped a hand to her head. "That's it! I'm so stupid."

CHAPTER 33

Horra wanted to kick herself. She should've known there'd be no bejeweled system for the hidden closet. It was the hook, set inside the fireplace a claw-length above the stone ledge and hidden. It resembled the passageway's triggers, except this one was polished and shiny. But now she had to get past the flames to trip it.

She stuck her claw in, but the hook was too far back, and the flames licked her hide. She cradled her arm against her chest. It was too far to reach without help. And she'd put in a good amount of wicker, enough to burn for longer than she wanted to wait. What could she use? She glanced around the room but found nothing.

She swung the knapsack from her shoulder, and it landed with a sound *thunk* on the floor. That was it! Horra dug through and found the dagger. It was the right length to reach the hook, but she had to twist it as well, which was hard to do with a slick blade. She was sweating by the time she managed to push the hook down far enough and open the latch.

The latch clicked, and a section of stone beside the

fireplace shifted and opened to reveal Woodsly's hiding place. The closet was as wide as her body and a head higher than she stood. It was stocked full of jars and containers with different kinds of ingredients.

She opened the Medicinal Curse Book to the antidote page and began shuffling through the ingredients for the ones she needed, stuffing them into her sack as she went. Soon, her knapsack was full, so she yanked one of the curtains off the bed and sat the rest of the items she needed on it.

She had everything except for two ingredients: snake oil and a plume from a plumy catterwump. Memories of the giant's house and the giant-sized catterwump that had chased her around the child's bedroom sent goosebumps along her hide.

"That catterwump would've created enough of a potion to free the whole of Oddar." Hopefully, there was still one in the lab to use. She gathered the items on the sheet, tied it into a bag, stomped out the embers that remained of the fire, and then remembered the fairies' words when she'd given them a tour. "Let them clean it up with their 'simple' spell."

The improvised sack and her knapsack were heavy, and her arms weakened from pain. Horra dragged the sheet across the floor to the door, wishing she could shrink them like she had shrunk herself and Pidge. She stopped and dug into the knapsack for the bag.

Both the cake and candy were smashed together. Possibly this would not do anything, but she had to try. She nibbled on a few crumbs of the cake to grow just enough to be able to get through the doors and ease the burden on her sore body.

Her stomach cramped, and she bent over waiting for it to pass. Tingles swept across her hide as she grew. The discomfort passed quickly, and though her clothes wore more like wearing a toddler's outfit, she hurried out of the quarters and ducked back into her father's suite.

Horra struggled to keep the jars from clanking and making too much noise, but luckily there were new, plush rugs everywhere to dull any sound. At least the fairies were good for something. She breathed easy when she pulled the sheet through the doorway and into the passage, securing the panel closed and sliding the bolt across to lock it.

"Whew! Getting around quick is so much easier when I'm bigger." She tugged at her waistband, which dug into her belly. The cold air nipped at her ankles. Good thing she'd lost some weight or it would be impossible to keep wearing them. However, she didn't have the time nor the clothes to change into to make her more comfortable.

Pidge flitted around, chasing after more vermin.

Horra considered where to find the remaining two ingredients and then where she would brew the potion. It had to be close to bedtime by now, and most creatures should be turning in soon.

Once inside the lab, Horra gathered the bowl and spatula and then searched the broken and jumbled containers for snake oil and a catterwump.

She found a glob of gelled snake oil on the floor next to its shattered glass jar and used the spatula to scrape it into a tin cup.

Pidge hunted while Horra searched and found an oil burner to place under the bowl. She'd finished setting up when she called Pidge. Her pet had an orange wiggling worm dangling from her beak. The pudge wudgie made quick work of gulping the insect down.

Horra rushed over to her, the broken glass crunching beneath her boots, and shoved the bird away. "Sorry, Pidge. It's life or death here." In the corner was the large square terrarium, which held different types of bugs. Horra reached in and grabbed two of the catterwumps while Pidge snapped at her. "I will get you the biggest one ever later. I promise."

She lined up the jars of ingredients, including the tin cup of snake oil and plumy catterwumps, and added the ingredients as per the recipe in the Medicinal Curse Book. When it came to the bugs, she could almost hear them squeal when she pulled off their plumes and added them to the bowl. Before she could apologize to the insects for essentially making them bald, Pidge swooped in and gobbled them up.

Horra placed her fists on her hips, almost sorry for the creatures. "Don't you ever get full?"

Pidge blinked her wide, golden eyes.

"You are not innocent, no matter how big those eyes are."

Several flicks of her sore claws later, she lit the burner. When the concoction came to a boil, she stirred it with the alderwood spatula three times right, five times left, and twice more right. Now it had to simmer until it turned clear, and then she had to cool it completely before she could use it on her father.

But she had to find her father to administer it. It couldn't be given in a shot. Troll hide was too thick except for their sharpest needles. And though there should've been a glut of them, she'd found none. It would therefore have to be ingested, either individually or added to something. Like food.

When the antidote's murky color cleared, she pulled it off the burner. Hazy light filtered through the windows on the lab's roof. Today was the day. She'd save her father from his wedding and then save her kingdom.

An explosion rocked the castle. Horra grabbed for the nearest counter to steady herself. Her pulse pounded in her veins.

Pidge squawked.

Jars, which had been on the counters and in the cupboards, rolled and shattered on the floor. The casting bowl tipped and rocked. Horra reached for it, but it was too late.

Her antidote spilled out and spread over the counter and dripped onto the floor.

CHAPTER 34

"No!" Horra cried out. Dismay crawled inside her heart and took up residence.

She grabbed the tin cup and raced over to the liquid oozing across the countertop. It burned her claws as she tried to scrape up as much of the liquid as she could, praying it would be enough.

Another explosion rocked the lab, and Horra slipped in some snake oil on the floor. The potion sloshed over the side of the cup, burning her claw.

What in dragon's fire was going on? Were they being invaded?

A third burst shattered some of the windows above Horra. Splinters of glass rained down, beating upon her backside as she bent over the cup. Thank goodness for the woodencloak's protection.

There was barely a dropper full of the antidote left. Horra jerked a drawer open and found a syringe and cap. She sucked up the liquid and capped it.

"C'mon, Pidge. We need to get to a safe place."

Horra grabbed her knapsack, put the syringe in the side pocket, and gathered the sack of ingredients in case she had time to make another potion. She teetered to the panel, her bundles making it awkward, and punched in the code. She tapped her boot impatiently until the door opened fully and she was able to pull everything through. Pidge fluttered past her.

The castle shuddered again, causing the panel to falter. The gears ground and caught but finally shut.

Bar in place to lock the door, Horra sank to the floor and set the knapsack next to her. She pictured her mother, her grandmother, and all of her foremothers. Oddar's fiercest protectors. They gave her courage enough to continue.

Rats and mice of all sizes raced around the passageway, seeking any safe place to hide, sending Pidge into a frenzy. Horra wished she could seek shelter as well, but she had to find out what was going on, and she had to find her father.

Boom!

Rocks and debris rained down on her. Pidge darted around in circles.

When the dust settled, Horra stood, lifted the knapsack to her shoulder, and headed to the kitchens, because if anyone knew what was going on, Sageel would.

Noises filtered through the storage room door. She pulled the hood of the woodencloak over her head, stuffed her wild tresses inside, and tugged on the lever.

The clinking and clanking of kitchen work grew in volume. Normally, the hobgoblins would be chattering, but there was no babble of voices. Horra shut the panel on Pidge, who flew toward her and screeched when the stone blocked her entry. There was no way to keep control of Pidge with her size now. Besides, if they were being invaded, the passageways were the safest place for her. No one would find her there, and her pet would have enough vermin to last a lifetime if something happened to her before she could return.

Horra gripped the knapsack tight and turned around, knocking a jug of something from the shelf. She caught it before it fell to the floor, but some of it spilled out of the cork and down the jug. "Snake oil. Of course! The hobgoblins use it for cooking." She wished she would've thought of it earlier, but she had enough for her father. That's all she needed for now.

She put the container back, wiped the oil off on her tunic, and stepped over to the open kitchen door. She'd hoped to overhear something that would let her know what was going on, but the hobgoblins raced around, oblivious to each other, silently bent on their duties.

A grand breakfast was being prepared, and by the scents, it was sweet and fruity. She'd almost rather eat a rat, but she longed to find something edible. Another explosion rocked the castle. Dust swirled in the air.

Horra snuck into the kitchen, hugging the wall on the far side—away from all of the activity. She glanced at her arm and realized the cloak blended in perfectly with the gray of the wall, just like Woodsly's gray exterior would've, but better. She relaxed and waited, watching.

As one, the hobgoblins stopped and gathered their trays and pitchers, and marched out of the kitchen, into the dining hall.

She hustled over to the icebox. Pink puddings and colorful juices with flowers floating in them sat inside. Candied berries and dainty vegetables drenched in a sweet syrup filled the rest of the space. There wasn't a stitch of meat or a root vegetable to be seen.

"How do they eat this stuff?" Horra flicked through the contents but found nothing that enticed her. Ends of bread loaves were in the trash container, so Horra pulled out two of the largest ones and dusted them off. She bit into them with fervor and located a pitcher of water without flowers to drink from.

Shuffling noises sounded from the hallway. Horra left the pitcher, ran into the darkness of the back wall, and prayed no one would notice a tree leaning against the stone surface.

Sageel and three other hobgoblins entered, carrying trays and pitchers.

More dust swirled and Horra sneezed.

The old hobgoblin's footsteps halted for a moment before she ducked her head and carried on. The others didn't notice Horra and kept up their duties without pause.

They bustled around. The three hobgoblins dumped out the remnants of their trays and pitchers, reloaded them with the items from the icebox, and left for the dining hall again. Sageel lingered behind.

She shoved her hearing aid back in her ear. "Princess?"

"Here," Horra called.

Sageel rushed over. She dug a chunk of wrapped meat out of her apron pocket. "Did you brew the antidote?"

"Yes. However, it spilled in the explosions. What's going on, and how did you see me?" She took a big bite, groaning with delight.

The servant laughed. "I didn't see you. I smelled you. You, princess, need a bath." Sageel's face turned grim. "They've blasted the wall your father built that blocked the chapel stairway. They plan to hold the ceremony there."

Horra choked on the meat. Her father was going to be remarried in their most holy place? Over her dead hide. "Not if I have anything to say about it." If only her father were the size of Pidge, she'd have enough of the antidote to un-mesmerize him.

That was it! She could shrink her father. But she'd need

Sageel's help. "I have a plan." She dug out the candy from the bag. "I just need to get this on my father's food. And then I need to add the antidote." She pulled out the syringe.

Sageel glanced over her shoulder toward the dining hall. "You'll have to hurry. The fairies don't eat much, and neither does you-know-who."

"Can you point me to my father's food? I can take care of the rest."

She pointed to a tray of gross-looking scraps. "There it is. But it's drugged. Best to dig something out of the garbage. You'll find him in the dungeon."

Horra faltered. "My father's in the dungeon?"

Sageel pulled a pitcher out of the icebox. "I have to go or they'll notice. Be careful, Princess. If they catch you, they won't be so kind this time around." The old hobgoblin hesitated. "And beware of the ballasts they brought in to eat up the rocky rubble. They're good and hungry, and they might mistake you for a boulder."

CHAPTER 35

Horra grabbed a bowl and a spoon to mash the candy. She dumped the rubbish from her father's tray and replaced it with scraps from the trash. She sprinkled the ground-up candy over the food and stirred it in for good measure. Then she dribbled the antidote across the food and headed to the dungeon.

Partway there, the familiar heavy footsteps of worqs lumbering down the hallway grit against the stone floor. The space was barely big enough for the worqs to walk side by side, let alone walk past her. She hurried back down the hall to where it forked off to the washroom.

Instantly, her nose started to run and her eyes itched.

Prickly powder!

Horra fought off the urge to sneeze. Setting the tray down, she moved into the bustling room. Laundress redcappers scrubbed multi-colored items, including leafy bedding. A couple of fancy dresses were hung that looked like they might be for the wedding. The redcappers were going to extremes to get the delicates ready for the special event.

That thought burned in her gut. The redcappers never took special care of her clothes. Except to add prickly powder and make her dresses as stiff as a winter wind across the mountains. She knew it was childish, but she couldn't help herself. When no one was looking, she sprinkled the hanging gauzy outfits with prickly powder and dumped a good amount into the wash water.

"That's for sentencing me and for killing all of my plants." She clapped the dust off of her hands and left the washroom.

She grabbed the tray and hurried back down the hall. Only three creatures, besides Sageel, had gone to the dungeon. Odds were on her side that no one else would come down.

The door into the dungeon was thick and heavy, and Horra had to set the tray down on the ground to open it. Two rats scurried over to the tray before she could pick it back up, and in moments, both convulsed and shrank.

"Serves you right!" Horra walked past the first cells and found her father slumped over in the cage next to Balk.

"Princess?" Balk asked.

Emotion clogged her throat and she cleared it. "I see you haven't broken out of here yet." She lowered the tray and checked her unmoving father for injuries.

"Not for lack of trying."

"Father? Wake up."

Balk grunted. "So that's who it is. Hasn't made a peep, that one. Did they drug him?"

"Sageel said they did." Horra shook the barred door and it swung open. She raced to her father and rolled him over. He groaned but didn't wake. His face appeared normal, but she didn't trust that the worqs hadn't done something to him she couldn't see.

She held some of the food by her father's nose. No reaction.

"He's not waking up."

"He's a big guy, huh? They leave the door open? Yeah, they drugged him good. They probably plan to give him something to wake up later for the wedding. Wait, did you bring us food?"

Horra glanced at the wall. "How do you know I have food?"

He laughed. "I have the nose of a hoarhound. I can smell anything. Including the contracting candy. You wouldn't have any extra, would you?"

"It's called contracting candy?" She tried to shove some food into the crease between her father's tusks and his lips. No success. "How do you know about contracting candy?"

"Ah, yes. The job I was doing before Floke die—disappeared was with the giants. I used it to shrink a rival elf so they could steal something valuable. Doesn't last long on giants, though. Only hours for the good stuff. Takes days to wear off on other creatures. Learned that one the hard way."

She shrugged. "Well, Pidge is back to her normal size, but I'm kind of in between. I was bigger when you found me."

"Hmm. Maybe it's different with trolls. I don't know any trolls who have ever tried contracting candy."

The dungeon doors squealed open. Horra grabbed the grub and rushed out of her father's cell and down the other end of the dungeon cells into the shadows.

Two worqs ambled into her father's cell, and with heavy grunts, picked him up, and carried him away. She punched the wall glad that the pain distracted her from tears that pricked the backs of her eyes. So close! How was she going to save him now?

With a defeated sigh she walked back to Balk's cell with the tray. "Well, dinner is served, giant's concoctions included."

Balk's eyes grew wide. He glanced around blindly. "Princess?"

Horra removed the hood and handed him the food.

"Your disguise is incredible! Probably worth a king's ransom." Balk spoke as he greedily gulped down the remaining food.

"It's not mine to give you, so don't ask." Horra glanced into other cells, but nobody moved. Her mind spun on what to do now. It was almost time to leave Oddar and get the seed to the Weald. And though the wedding today wouldn't affect her kingdom, thanks to Balk's quick thinking, she still couldn't leave without trying to make the potion once more.

Maybe she could slip it into the wedding meal so that the whole of the wedding party would become un-mesmerized. She had to at least try. If she couldn't get another potion made, she'd leave tonight as promised.

Balk shook and collapsed. In a flash, he was small enough that the shackles fell off and he could walk through the bars. He glanced down and laughed.

"Got any of their expanding desserts?" Balk winked at her. "Learned that one the hard way, too."

She found the bag and gave him some. "My supply is dwindling."

Balk grew back to his original size. He glanced into her father's cell and frowned. "Now what, Princess?"

Horra gnawed on an uneven clawnail. "I have to try to get another potion made. At least you'll be un-mesmerized no matter what."

Balk glanced around. "What about them?"

Horra hesitated. She wanted everyone freed, but that would give her away. "I don't think we can until I have the potion made. Then it'll be safe to get them out."

"Whatever you say. But, can we get out of here before our worqen host returns and finds us?"

Horra couldn't take him in the passages. The only other

alternative was through the hallway to the door that led to the stables.

"Take my hand."

She flipped her hood back over her head and adjusted her hair, then peeked through the heavy door. It creaked enough to put her on edge. No one was in the hallway. They hurried down, past the laundry, and to the door near the kitchen. The hobgoblins were busy, so she peered out the door.

It was clear.

Together, they ran over to the last stable where Nimble was kept. Inside, it was silent. Horra patted Nimble's snout as Balk walked around, scouting everything.

"I need to get to my supplies for the antidote. I'll be back." She met his gaze. "Don't do anything while I'm gone."

CHAPTER 36

"I'm back," Horra announced to Balk. She was surprised to find him sitting on a bale of hay, whittling. "Where did you find a knife?"

Since she couldn't use the passageway, she'd gone back through the kitchen and slipped into the passages to get the bag full of ingredients. She'd used the cloak for her and Pidge on the way out.

"Metalmagic, remember?"

"I need to work fast." She laid out all of the ingredients and realized the bowl was not going to be big enough. "Balk? Do you know what else I can use as a bigger casting bowl?"

He grunted. "Don't need that if you got the right gems."

"What do you mean?"

"Do you still have your dagger?" His face was serious.

She retrieved it from the bag.

"Now I use my Creature God given talents." He chanted.

The hilt glowed. Startled, Horra dropped it. When it landed, the gems fell out of the handle. "What was that for?"

"I can reset them, Princess. Just place the sapphires and

rubies at the top and the emeralds and diamonds at the opposite end."

She did as he requested.

Balk chanted again, and the bowl grew to pot size. "Don't move the gems, or the bowl will return to its original size."

Horra nodded and, with the Medicinal Curse book open to the correct page, began. When it came time to heat the liquid, she had to use the burner on full blast and a flame on both of her claws to heat it.

"Princess, I think they realized I'm missing." Balk spoke while watching the castle.

She blew on her fingers to accentuate the flame. "The liquid has to be clear. It's not clear yet."

Nimble whinnied and stomped its feet.

"They're heading this way, Princess. They're at the stables in front of us."

Horra put her free hand on one of the pillars. "Kryk. Can you hear me?"

The wood split and formed a face. "Yes, Princess."

Pidge squealed and landed on the wood. She fluffed her feathers and preened herself.

"Are you able to hide us or keep them from coming in? I have a plan, but the potion isn't ready yet." Her voice cracked.

The barn creaked and the air snapped around them. "You need to hurry, Princess. You must leave before nightfall, or you won't get to the Weald in time."

"If everything goes as planned, I will be ready."

Kryk disappeared. Voices sounded from outside of the stable. Horra held her breath, and Balk remained silent as he stared out of the window.

The potion was changing from dark to murky.

Balk laughed. "They're leaving. I knew you were special the moment I saw you in that alley, Princess. But to be protected by the Forest Roods? You're Nomans'—no, the Wilden Land's—greatest warrior." He bowed.

"Not if I don't save my kingdom and get to the Weald, I'm not." Horra blew on her claws again, and the potion boiled fully and finally cleared. "Balk, I need a bucket."

He gave her a wooden bucket, and she poured the antidote into it. "Balk—"

The bocan held his hands up. "I know. I know. Stay here and stay hidden."

She smiled. "It won't be long now. Can you keep an eye on Pidge, please?" She hefted the bucket up. "Balk? You're a better Champion Bearer than I thought you'd be. Your daughter would be proud."

Tears glistened in his eyes. "Thank you, Princess."

Horra hustled to the castle. The kitchen was in chaos. She waited to catch sight of Sageel. Several of the hobgoblins wore pastel-colored uniforms, while others wore the same old outfits.

Sugared rose petals adorned a dozen golden, baked swans on the table. Pastel-colored fruit filled the largest trays. Blue juice sparkled in grand glass decanters she'd never seen before. A hobgoblin dressed in a frosty pink uniform tasted the juice, nodded, and placed the cup next to the decanter.

Horra worked her way along the wall to get close enough to the food to add the antidote. She grabbed the cup the hobgoblin had used and dipped it into the bucket she carried, dumping the antidote into the pitchers. She worked quickly, always keeping an eye out in case anyone noticed her, but none of them did.

Hobgoblins lined up and carried the fruit trays out first. Others lined up dessert bowls for a creamy pudding the cook stirred at the stove. Horra dumped the remainder of the antidote into the pudding when the cook turned away.

She wondered how fast the potion would work. The

servants returned to get the swans, juice, and pudding. Horra slipped along the wall to the serving room in between the kitchen and the dining room and poked her head out to see what was happening.

The dining room had been magicked into a room as large as the Conservatory. Several hundred creatures were seated at round tables across the room. At the end of the room was the rectangular royal table. Tinkling music filled the room.

There, sitting at the head of the table, was her father in his flitterfly-colored suit. He was dazed, sleepy even. She silently prayed that the antidote would override any of the other drugs they'd given him.

On her father's left was the fairy queen, looking gauzy in a sparkling, fuzzberry-shaded dress, the color matching her diaphanous wings. Her skin had a bright pink tint to it. Her daughters sat to her left, looking just as bright pink as their mother. One wore a glittering, frizzlebug-colored dress with feathers, and the other wore a shimmery, fruit-beetle-shaded gown, each matching their wings.

Though they wore colorful attire, the air around them didn't coalesce or glow. A dullness that muted their beauty settled around them like a storm cloud.

Horra realized with some satisfaction that the fairies tried inconspicuously to scratch ... everywhere. Frown lines creased their painted lips. Maybe she wouldn't outlaw prickly powder after all.

On her father's right was the Erlking. He was the only one in attendance not wearing a pastel-colored outfit. His black robe and grey skin stood out among the crowd.

Down the table and next to a pretty fairy she didn't recognize sat Torren. She narrowed her eyes at him. He was less animated than usual. The fairy talked and laughed, but

Torren barely cracked a smile. His face was shadowed and creased instead of smooth and youthful.

Though the hobgoblins in the hamlet she'd visited didn't seem to be present, there were numerous hobgoblins here. They wore outlandishly hued outfits, some of the fabric she remembered from Filbus's table. She'd rather wear her torn and disgusting clothes.

She leaned back out of the way as the pastel-bedecked servants filed through the doorway with the trays holding the carved swans. Sweet scents swirled after them. Glasses were filled to the brim with the blue juice.

She slipped back into the kitchen and through the passage. She needed to stock up on weapons while they ate. If the antidote didn't work, she still needed to protect herself on the way to the Weald. And she needed to get Balk something a metalsmith would appreciate.

The passages didn't lead to the armory, so she had to go through the Hall of Monstrosity. Canvases and wooden frames lay in smashed ruins on the floor. Their prized stuffed swamp swine's horns were broken, the stuffing strewn about. Horra stood, speechless.

CHAPTER 37

Broken and battered, her great, great, great, great grandmother's portrait lay on the floor, staring up at her. Her eyes held a determination and courage Horra didn't feel. Across the room, her mother's portrait was slashed, but her expression held the same strength of will. They were larger than life, even after death. Even with their portraits in tatters on the ground. Their legacy couldn't be undone. It was alive and well in her blood, and her heart, flawed as it was.

Anger, hot and swift, burned from the top of her red head to her boots. Horra was a part of these women. These fierce and fabulous warriors. At this moment she claimed it.

She could do this. She wouldn't let them down.

Horra hurried past toppled statues and through a hidden side door to the armory. It had been ransacked as well. Only a few swords and bows lined the walls, with one remaining quiver and several arrows unbroken but strewn across the room. She grabbed the bow and arrows, a belt, and a sharp sword for Balk. She stuck a smaller, jeweled dagger in her boot.

She slipped back into the hall, refusing to look at the carnage, and returned through the passage to the kitchen. Hobgoblins still scurried around, carrying trays of empty plates and glasses.

Had the antidote worked? What in piggle's feet would she do if it didn't?

She snuck past the servants to the doorway to see if the potion had begun to work.

The Erlking clinked a spoon against his goblet. "A toast to the royal couple."

Everyone took a drink of the blue juice. Including Torren, who downed his.

"Now, time for the ceremony." The Erlking lead the way. The hood covered his disturbing face, and only his bony hands showed beneath the full sleeves of his cloak. Her father stood unsteadily and held his claw out to the fairy queen, who didn't hesitate to take it. They walked regally out of the dining hall and into the grand hallway.

Where was Sageel? Horra slipped out of the serving hall and into the dining room, careful to avoid any of the hobgoblins. When the last of the guests filtered out of the room, Horra followed at a distance.

Rubble littered the hallway where her father's wall had been blown open earlier that day. It had been a ghastly barrier made of huge stone squares that blocked a grand marble stairway. It was blasted apart with chunks of stone lying everywhere. Ballasts, large boulder-like creatures, scoured the area, eating the largest rocks as the guests strode up the surprisingly clean carpet-lined steps.

She hadn't seen that stairway for so long, she stopped and stared for a moment. Memories of playing on the steps when she was younger, chasing her mother up and down them, or sitting and reading at the top of the stairs where there were cushioned benches pinched her heart.

Horra turned away to keep from reliving them. It was too painful. She hung back, as much from not wanting to be seen as not wanting to see the intruders inside her precious chapel.

Something bumped into Horra, and she realized one of the ballasts was feeling around for more rocks. Ballasts were rocks and dust held together by a primitive spell like their cousins the golems. She darted away just before it gathered a large stone she'd been standing by. It bit down, splattering chunks of rock everywhere.

A couple of the guests glanced around and then gazed at each other curiously. They stopped and let other guests go by.

By the time the last of the procession reached the second floor, some started to stagger, their faces creased as if confused. Their voices were less animated.

One particularly regal female fairy stopped, turned, and said something Horra couldn't hear. She stood near a male troll who was shaking his head. He bumped into her, and the fairy's face twisted in anger. She screamed at the troll. The troll, in turn, yelled back. Screaming and chaos erupted.

This was getting out of control too fast. But where was the Erlking? Where was her father?

The ballast Horra'd just escaped from drew closer, and she moved against the wall, nearer to the stairs. She waited for an opportunity to step in, but spells and curses rent the air with snapping flashes of light. The troll dug at a sticky substance across his mouth. The regal fairy smiled down over him. Two trolls rushed the fairy, who then disappeared in a glittery flourish.

Horra shivered. This was worse than the few Goblin Court altercations she'd witnessed in the past. Had she done something wrong with the antidote? Or was this simply the crowd waking from the spell?

Shrieks rent the air. The colorful guests darted down the stairs while sparks and sparkles followed them. They charged through to the dining room. A scent, crossed between sweetsuckle and sulfur, filled the air.

Horra was rushed. Despite her disguise, the crowd jostled her around. A troll ran by, arms flailing, his colorful suit aflame, knocking her to the floor. Horra curled up in a ball to keep from being trampled, rolling out of the way once the majority of the horde was gone.

Spells, both sparkling and smoky, whizzed down the grand staircase. The noise from the screaming ebbed as the guests filed out, away from the chaos. Horra stood.

The Erlking stumbled down the stairs dodging glittering spells, the royal fairies close behind. And they were angry. They faced off, sending spells at each other, most deflected, leaving burning marks wherever they landed. The blonde fairy princess—Horra couldn't recall if she were Misty or Glory—screamed and sent a sphere of fire toward the Erlking It hit his chest, catching his cape ablaze. A tinny note hung in the air and then ended. The Erlking grabbed at a hidden pocket and removed a charred pan flute.

"That's for mesmerizing me," the blonde fairy shrieked. "This is for all the things you made me do while I was under your control." She circled her hands above her head.

The Erlking flicked his wrists and sent a black, smoldering ball at her. It landed squarely between her eyes, sending her airborne. A trail of smoke followed her as she tumbled down the stairs. Her body lay still and broken at the bottom of the staircase.

Horra stifled a scream, a hand clutched to her mouth.

The queen's face distorted with fury and her pink-tinged

skin deepened to red. The brunette fairy and two fairy guards rushed to the blonde's side. The queen gripped her staff and its pearl whorled a gray-white color. A twinkle of magic spun from its center, grew, and flashed toward the Erlking.

He moved but the spell blew his hood from his head. Black veins beat furiously beneath semitransparent skin. His pale lips were twisted in a grimace. His sunken eyes were glistening ebony stones. Long, stringy, gray strands hung from his scalp. However, most shocking were the puckered scars where his ears should have been.

Horra stared at the Erlking's grotesque head. She recalled Balk's story of the elves cutting the ears off of their rogue dark magic-using brethren. She'd never seen anything so abominable. She couldn't tear her eyes away. Fear, the truest kind she'd ever experienced, pumped through her veins.

Her father staggered down the staircase. He yanked at the silky tie around his neck, tossing it off. Hope filled Horra. Was he back? Had the antidote overcome the other drugs?

The furious queen drove the Erlking down the staircase to the landing on the second floor. Luminous white spells zinged from the queen's staff. They were countered by dark, vaporous curses from the Erlking. Back and forth, they attacked. However, the Erlking was fast. One of the spells ricocheted and hit Horra directly in her knapsack.

She flew backward and hit the wall behind her, smacking her head and knocking the air out of her. Horra struggled to inhale. When she could finally breathe, she wished she could throw a spell back at the Erlking. One that would turn him into the rat he was so she could feed him to Pidge.

As if on cue, Pidge fluttered around the stairway above her. That could only mean one thing.

Balk ran into the hallway. "Horra! Where are you?"

"Horra?" Her father shouted her name above the magic

flashing back and forth. He rushed down the stairway, dodging the whizzing magic spells and burning curses.

"Where are you, my daughter?" His gaze traveled over and then past her, not seeing her.

Had they blinded him?

CHAPTER 38

The horror at the thought of her strong father being blind ricocheted through her. She clenched her fists. "I'm here, Father." She panted in quick, shallow puffs. Her head throbbed where it had hit the stone wall, her eyesight dotted with sparks of light.

The ballast was close by her again, having ingested all of the bigger stones nearby. Pidge swooped down, distracting it.

"Be careful, Pidge!" she yelled as she crawled away, trying to get to the king. Another spell hit the wall behind her, sending piercing shards of stone everywhere. She ducked into a ball, covering her head.

"Where are you?" the king called. "Horra!"

Horra realized the woodencloak had become gray and blended in with the stone walls. She grabbed the hood and yanked it down, uncovering her head.

With a relieved cry, her father ran to her, but the ballast got there first. It grabbed her and lifted her to its mouth. Flashes of the giant child crossed her mind, and she screamed.

King Divitri swung his fist at the rock beast and knocked a large boulder out of its center.

Its gravelly squeal hurt Horra's ears. She closed her eyes and wrapped her arms around her head.

The king swung again and knocked the beast backward. "Let go of the princess!" he shouted. His last punch cracked it fully, breaking it in half.

It dropped Horra and toppled into a large pile of rubble. Other ballasts hurried over to the smashed rock and devoured it in seconds.

Pidge darted after something, on the hunt again.

Horra rushed to her father and hugged him.

He stood motionless for a moment and then returned the embrace. "My daughter! You're safe!"

It only lasted a couple of moments before they were both uncomfortable. Horra stepped back. "We're not completely safe yet." She handed her father the sword she'd taken from the Armory. "Balk!" she yelled and tossed him the small dagger.

She could see questions in her father's gaze, but she turned and headed toward the action. Toward the Erlking.

The ballasts had finished eating the rubble and instead were intent on beating each other and eating the pieces that they knocked free. The massive door troll broke away from the crowd and started to beat the remaining creatures to a pulp. Dust flew everywhere.

A flash lit up the area and her father ducked to cover Horra. His posture tightened, and he gestured to the bocan. "I don't know who you are, but let's end this."

Balk pulled out her mother's dagger. "Hope you don't mind, Princess. I put it back together again." He threw it to her. "Remember my vision?"

She removed the cloak. "I do."

"Make it happen." Without waiting for Horra to respond,

Balk dashed up the stairs toward the fairies. They were on the second floor and the only way to go was toward the Grand Library's walkway.

Her father strode, taking the steps two at a time, past Balk and the fairies to the third floor, which led to the chapel.

Emboldened by the presence of her father and Balk, Horra nocked an arrow and aimed. It went left, past the Erlking's head as he sent off a hex at the queen. The hex pitched left and hit the ceiling. A chunk of stone dropped and fell to the stairs, rolling down to the hallway.

He jerked his gaunt face toward her and scowled. Quick as a blink, a blue, funnel-shaped curse with lightning flashing from the center appeared in his palm. Balk rushed to attack, slicing the Erlking across his thigh. The curse dropped to the stairs, igniting the carpet. Sapphire flames spread across the floor.

She nocked a new arrow, corrected her aim, and sent it flying. It struck the Erlking in his shoulder. Black oozed down his cloak. He screamed in agony, conjured a smoldering, gray ball, and flung it at her. Horra ducked and rolled like Woodsly had taught her in defense class.

Her father returned from the chapel, dragging an unconscious Torren by his iridescent cape. The king laid him down on a step and produced a golden sword, Oddar's ceremonial sword. It was the only sword in Oddar forged with the ability to negate the magic of its victims. Horra smiled at the sight.

Two fairy guards joined the queen, and working together, they created a silver, crackling sphere. It grew until it was as big as Pidge. Together they sent it spiraling toward the Erlking as King Divitri and Balk charged. Horra nocked another arrow, but before she could release it, the Erlking retreated, running toward the walkway.

"He's headed toward the library, Father," Horra yelled. She jumped over the brunette fairy leaning over her blonde sister and ran up the stairs after the others, following the Erlking.

The sun dipped low and lit the glass windows of the library with yellow-orange light. The view of the Iron Mountains outside was a vibrant sight, and the snow on the tops sparkled as if magic themselves. The Erlking ran across the walkway maze built above the library. The alabaster, carved walls reflected the glowing sunset, making the area radiate like a spotlight.

There was no way out for the Erlking unless he climbed to the library below. And they'd catch him before that.

The fairies, rushing onto the walkway, sent a burst of netted magic at him, but the trap fell short and fizzled out on the swampwood bookshelves.

Her father and Balk raced across different paths of the walkway.

Horra knew exactly how to cut the Erlking off. She stuck the dagger in her mouth and took a shortcut toward him, along the ledge of the library wall which was lined with historical relics and priceless war artifacts. She'd sometimes done it late at night, just for fun. She knew where to step, and how to get across quicker than going the long way.

Clinging to the carved stone walls, she shuffled along the shelf, trying to avoid all of the items. Her boot bumped a large vase depicting the War of the Warts, and it fell to the floor and shattered into pieces. Undeterred, she kept moving until she reached the center of the walkway which intersected the ledge.

She ran across the path and cornered the Erlking above the magical creatures section along the windowed side, the jeweled dagger in her hand. Maybe Balk's dream would come true.

She sneered at him. Her heart raced, and she was breathing

hard. "You can't get away. I'll make it gentle like your worqs did." She pointed the dagger at him.

Her father and Balk closed in behind her. Balk chuckled.

"Oh, but I can, Princess. This isn't over, though. I'll see you again." The Erlking jumped, sending a spell before him to break the outer glass window. He dropped two stories to the ground.

Horra rushed to the shattered window and glanced down. Panicked, she scanned the area. "Where is he? Where'd he go?" It couldn't be! She'd had him right in front of her. There was no way anyone could survive that kind of fall. No one could.

But there was no body, no sign of the Erlking below.

It was as if he'd completely disappeared.

CHAPTER 39

Horra stared at the ground in disbelief. "No! He was right there—"

Her father engulfed her in an embrace. The second one of the evening, it surprised her more than the Erlking's disappearance. The king's burly arms clung to her tight. "I'm so glad you're all right, daughter."

Horra patted him on the back. For three years, she'd longed to have this again. It was as strange as it was enjoyable. A strange warmth and relief spread through her chest. "You, too, father."

The queen cleared her throat and faced them. "King Divitri, Princess Horra, I extend my deepest apologies for everything that has occurred since ..." A sob broke from her dainty lips.

Her daughter moved to take her mother's hand. Waning sunlight threw a halo around them once again, though it wasn't bright as much as sad, now that they were free from the Erlking's spell. "We will make it up to you both." She struck a fist to her chest.

Surprise rocketed Horra. It was a rare show of honor, especially after their previous, though mesmerized, actions. Kryk's words came back to her. Did she seek revenge or forgiveness? Her anger lessened. It was the Erlking, after all, who was the mastermind, not the fairies.

She faced the queen, a broken woman, and dipped her head and moved her right claw in the fairy tradition of welcome and acceptance. It was strange, and Horra hoped it was correct since she'd never actually done it before.

The fairy queen bowed her head and waved her hand back.

The king took a deep breath and mimicked Horra's actions. "Apology accepted. I, too, succumbed to the Erlking's ploys."

The queen wept bitter tears, her teary-eyed daughter beside her as they retraced their steps back toward the staircase where the other princess lay battered among the rubble on the stairs.

Balk waited at the bottom of the stairs to walk beside her. "Princess. You have to leave."

The king stopped and gave her a surprised look. "Leave? You're not leaving."

Pidge landed next to Horra, a rodent in her ebony beak. Happiness flittered in her stomach at the sight of the feather on top of the bird's glorious head which Horra had broken off in their flight from the castle. It was growing again. She scratched the bird's neck. "You have to stay here, girl. Get rid of all of those rats."

"Why do you think you're leaving?" her father demanded. "We've much to do to get the kingdom back in order."

The queen gracefully kneeled beside her daughters. "She's still alive, but only just." The blonde lay on her side, facing away from them on the floor. The queen's hands glowed with pearlescent light, but the princess didn't move.

Horra's heart pricked for the girl. No matter how friffity the fairy was, she hadn't deserved this. The Erlking had to be stopped. Horra couldn't let him get away with all this destruction, but she had to get to the Weald first.

"I have much to do as well, father. I have a mission to take Woodsly's seed to the Weald to regenerate. But I'm almost out of time. If I don't get there in two days, it will die. It's our only hope of defeating the Erlking."

Her father hovered over her. "We can send another to take the seed."

Horra shook her head. "It's too important. The roods said it had to be me."

The fairy queen and brunette princess gasped, their dainty hands held to their petite mouths in surprise.

Her father gaped. "Roods? You spoke with the roods?"

Balk stepped up to them. "It's true. I saw it with my own eyes. They kept your daughter safe in the stables so she could get the antidote to everyone."

Emotions warred across her father's face. "Who are you, bocan?" He ground the last word out but managed not to make it a snarl.

He bowed. "Balk, your Majesty. I served your daughter in your absence. I pledge my help to you and your kingdom."

Her father grunted. "I see. You have my gratitude." He turned to Horra. "But, you're so young. Are you ready for such a big mission?"

"Looks like your daughter can handle quite a bit." The queen smiled at Horra. "You single-handedly saved us, didn't you?"

"Not without help." Horra nodded to Balk.

"Sometimes we don't know what we can do until we are forced to do it." The queen put a fist to her chest and bowed her head. Another show of honor? Her opinion of the fairies continued to change. The queen scratched at her neck. The skin there was still spotted and pink from a rash.

Guilt pricked her conscience. "You may need some ointment your guards used in the Conservatory for your prickly powder rash." She turned to her father. "I truly need to go."

Torren roused, grunting.

She frowned. "What will you do with him?"

The king shooed her away. "I will see to him. Go."

Her knapsack was charred, ruined from the Erlking's curse. She dug the seed out to make sure it was okay. The black spot had grown. She tried to wipe it off but couldn't. A sense of dread overtook her. "I need to hurry."

"It would be my honor to accompany you, my lady, and keep you safe." Balk bent and thumped his chest with a fist. "If that is acceptable to you, your highness? It was the Erlking who killed my daughter, after all."

Her father studied them back and forth. "What say you, daughter? Is he trustworthy?"

Horra grinned. "As trustworthy as anyone I know at the moment. Besides, he is prone to a good deal."

Balk's mouth opened and then shut. "I hope you're not near as shrewd as your daughter, sir."

Her father held out the golden sword. "I agree that Balk will be recognized as an official escort for the princess's safety. You shall return my daughter to me whole and unassaulted, and I will pay you fifty gold bars and arm you with weapons and supplies needed to take on your journey. If you fail, you will forfeit your life. May it be?" He cut his palm.

Balk grasped the golden sword's edge, slicing his hand. "May it be."

A blast of golden light sealed the deal.

"Balk, we need to find two animals strong enough to get us there quickly." Horra hurried toward the kitchen.

Balk held a hand up. "Sageel helped me get everything set up already, Princess. Go get cleaned up before you catch the crud. Is there anything you need?"

Crud? She definitely didn't want that. "Food and drink. I'm starving, so bring lots of it."

Balk saluted and departed.

The brunette fairy cleared her throat. "You'll find your belongings in the storage room beside the washroom." Her smile was apologetic.

Horra nodded and ran upstairs. At least the fairies were neat. Everything from her father's room, the instructor's quarters, and her room was piled neatly against a wall. She spied a knapsack on top of Woodsly's belongings.

Her clothes were too small now. Rummaging around, she found some of her mother's old outfits. She held them to her nose and could still smell the minty musk that was her mother's scent. Her mouth twisted in a half-smile, half-frown as tears pricked her eyes.

She didn't have time to reminisce long, though. Her heart twisted as she grabbed a new set of clothes from her mother's pile—a skirt that was also pants, and a blouse. Her cold shower was lighting fast but sufficient to wash her off.

She braided her wet hair and tied it back with a ribbon before hurrying back downstairs.

There, she stuffed the contents from her ruined knapsack into the new one, including her mother's bejeweled dagger, and folded the woodencloak on top for easy access. The seed she put in her pants pocket for safekeeping.

The fairy queen and the brunette princess were tending to the blonde princess, murmuring spell after spell over her corpse-like figure. When the brunette pushed a lock of golden hair away from her sister's face, Horra bit back a gasp.

Hair stuck out of her ears, and lumpy growths dotted her

face, arms, and hands. The blonde fairy's once-petite face was swollen and disfigured. One eye was lower than the other, and they were now as large as a gulpy's.

Compassion rocked her. She sent up a silent prayer of healing but, not wanting to disturb their ministrations, rushed by them toward the kitchen.

The hobgoblins had gathered two loaves of bracken bread with bacon grease and two flasks each of water and juice. She spied trash cans filled with candied food.

She met Balk at the stables. "Where is Sageel? I'd like to thank her."

"She saved us two beasts. She's busy cleaning up after everything. She sent her regards."

Horra's father strode over. "Ready to go?"

"Yes."

"Be safe." He gave her a bag of coins. His eyes perused her from head to toe. "You've grown overnight."

Warmth spread from her chest. "You've no idea. Thank you, father."

He grabbed her in a tight hug and kissed the top of her wet head. Three times in one day? Horra wasn't sure how to act.

Tears glistened in her father's eyes. "Remember your oath."

Balk nodded. He helped Horra onto Nimble's back between the wings where her mother's old saddle was strapped, then mounted one of his Stempners. Unlike the calm Nimble, it jittered sideways, unsure of its rider.

"Let's get this seed to the Weald." Horra grinned.

CHAPTER 40

Bright moonlight lit their path. Horra followed Balk on his massive steed. Though she was fairly certain the Weald would reveal itself, she let Balk lead because of his experience.

They stopped outside of Bough Valley the next morning to rest and feed their animals.

"There's something I need to do. I'll be back shortly." Horra marched toward the market.

The peddler section was just opening. Lines of tables displayed various wares. She stopped at the baker's table and asked for a sour bun. She overpaid the woman, assuring her it was a tip for the wonderful-smelling delicacy.

At the butcher's table, she bought some jerky and again overpaid, thanking the man for his finely crafted meat.

"Thank you, Princess."

She glanced at him, wide-eyed. "How did you—"

"You're beautiful, just like your mother was. It's my honor to serve you." He thumped a fist to his chest. "Please send our best regards to your father. We are so glad to hear the ceremony did not go off quite as planned, hmmm."

"Thank you, good sir." Horra walked away smiling. No one had ever called her beautiful before. She liked it.

Balk sat with a goblet of mead in his hands. His dark hair on the shaved side grew to cover his tattooed head. His flattened nose peaked out over a bush of a beard. Though not as scary as before, he was intimidating even as he sat casually beside his horse.

She tossed him a chunk of the jerky, then tore the bun in half and gave a piece to him.

"You're awfully cheery. Did you visit a beau?" He bit into the bun, a sarcastic grin on his tired face.

She shrugged. "I kind of pilfered some food while I was on my way to the castle. I vowed I'd return and pay them back. The butcher recognized me because of my hair."

She sipped the juice in her canteen and chewed on the bun. Several of the hobgoblins glanced her way and gossiped openly about the failed wedding.

"Word travels fast. Would you like me to defend your honor?"

She sent him an exasperated look. "You'd only give them something more to talk about." She took another sip of juice.

Balk grunted. "Maybe it wasn't such a great idea to stop here so soon after the Erlking disappeared. He won't give up, you know. You heard him. He'll be back."

Her stomach churned and she put the jerky away for later. "I heard what he said." She bumped his arm. "But your prophecy was wrong. I didn't get close to having the dagger held to his throat."

He frowned and shrugged. "Perhaps that wasn't when the vision was supposed to happen. You'll still have your chance, And I'm not giving up on finding my daughter."

Horra shrugged, still unsure if the vision of his daughter being alive was true. "Just don't expect me to believe in the vision you had of me. I don't believe in visions." She didn't tell him about the vision she'd had about her mother while jailed.

"Well, Princess, you don't have to believe for them to come true. Are you ready to leave?"

Horra gathered her items and packed them in the saddlebag. "Let's go."

They traveled over Hobgoblin Pass, a bridge that spanned a large river below, which connected the dwarf, troll, and hobgoblin lands. Built by giants, it was several wagon lengths wide, cut from the thick stone at the mountain's base. Table-sized boulders created the bridge's sides. It was tall enough to keep anyone from tumbling down to the water below.

"When we get to the other side of the Pass, keep on your toes. That is where the dark elves come out to play. It's called the Riven for a reason. It's a place of dark magic and evil. Even my informant elf was afraid to go there." Balk spat on the ground.

"How long has it been there, and where are its borders?" Horra asked.

"Don't know. I heard whispers in that market that more children have gone missing." Balk's stare was haunted. He blinked and it was gone. "We should be safe if we stay on the path."

Horra glanced at the other travelers. It was busy today, with numerous buggies, carts, and peddlers selling their wares before winter complicated traveling.

Balk narrowed his eyes and stared off at the horizon, possibly the direction of the Weald. Everyone knew about where it was, but it never revealed itself unless you were invited in. So you could travel around in circles and never find it. "Keep close. Don't get separated from me until we reach the Weald."

She snorted. "You just want the reward."

"Oh, I want the reward, all right. But something hasn't felt right since we left Bough Valley." His Stempner whinnied and high-stepped.

Spooked, Nimble belched and flapped its bony wings.

The last thing she needed was a gulgoyle going rogue. Horra clenched the reins and patted its neck. "Good Nimble! You almost had some smoke come out of your nose!" Twisting in the saddle, she turned toward Balk and asked in an overly calm voice. "What is it?"

He glanced around at the crowded pass and beyond. His leather gloves rasped as he gripped the dwarfen sword her father had given him. It hummed in his hands and glowed with a low radiance. "Hmmm. I couldn't say, but my intuition is never wrong. Danger is nearby. Be on alert."

Be on alert—the same admonition that Woodsly had given her in his letter. And Woodsly hadn't ever been wrong, either. Unease knotted her stomach.

However, Nimble had only been accustomed to her mother as a rider, which had been years ago, and the gulgoyle was undernourished. Though they were a stout beast, being a mixed breed of gully dragon and gargoyle, Horra didn't want to push it too hard.

Both Nimble and Balk's steed jerked their heads and faltered. Other horses around them became alarmed.

"Now, Princess." Balk prodded his horse.

Horra grabbed the jeweled dagger and kicked Nimble into a run.

CHAPTER 41

Something whizzed by Horra's ear and landed with a crash against the bridge. Rocks flew in every direction.

Nimble's eyes lit up with fear, its bare wings wide as if the beast wanted to fly.

Horra tugged at the reins to keep it under control. She was unused to riding, let alone being atop a panicked beast. She tried not to let her fear show, knowing the gulgoyle could sense it. But it was impossible for her not to when they were running at full speed.

She glanced around to find Balk. He rode behind her, the Stempner blowing out great heaving breaths as it dashed. On the other side of the bridge, where they had entered, was a bespeckled giant. It was furry, with a menacing scowl on its face. It threw boulders at a group of people who were attacking it.

Horra recognized the giant's voice and attire. It was the giant girl, Grendel. Is this what had been happening when she escaped the giant house? Her tusks ground together.

Another boulder rolled down the bridge, leaving a line

deeply scratched in the stone as it rolled, headed right for them. It knocked several creatures aside and smashed others beneath its weight.

Horra yanked the reins left, and Balk followed her lead. They were at the end of the bridge. It was now crowded with people rushing away from the danger.

"Nimble, I wish you had feathers." She pulled back on the straps to keep the gulgoyle from trampling a gnome family and their goats, which were pulling a miniature wagon. Her arms screamed with pain as she pulled with all of her might against Nimble's strong lead.

The rock crashed into the bridge, knocking a hole in the side. Screams followed the creatures that fell to the side and below. More panic erupted.

Horra pulled Nimble to the right and, with mighty jumps, reached the end of the bridge.

Once off of the bridge, they raced through the countryside, always staying close to the road. Finally, Nimble showed signs of weakening, and Horra slowed it down to a walk. Balk joined her.

"Did you see that?" she asked him, breathless.

"Probably won't get that image out of my mind in this lifetime." He glanced behind him. "I think we lost the giant."

"I think I know who that was." She shook her head and patted Nimble's neck.

"Giants all look the same. Are you sure you recognized them?"

Horra frowned. "I'm sure."

He pointed to a path to the side. "Let's get these beasts watered before they collapse."

They stopped at a place along the road to rest. Horra couldn't sit, though. She knew it was Grendel. She remembered the music. If only she'd gotten the Erlking in the maze.

Still, it wouldn't have stopped Grendel's change. What kind of magic changed someone that fully? The princess's face came to mind. Jitters shook her body.

"You're making me nervous," Balk said over his flask.

She paced back and forth and clutched the seed in her pocket. "I can't help it. How much farther do we have to go?"

He squinted at the sky. "We'll make it by nightfall if we're earnest. You probably should eat something." He handed her a piece of jerky.

"What're we waiting for?" She tore at the jerky instead of eating it. She couldn't stomach anything.

"We're trying not to kill the only transport we have."

She flopped to the ground, head on her knees. Her hair had come loose from her tie, so she redid it.

"You talk to roods, stood up to an evil Erlking, but you're afraid of a little wooly giant." Balk chuckled.

"It wasn't little. It had fangs, and claws, and everything." How powerful was the Erlking? Why had he targeted Grendel? Horra stood and paced again.

"You have fangs—actually, you have tusks now. *And* you have claws."

She made a face at him. But she couldn't help but beam slightly at the acknowledgment of her tusks.

"All right. I'm sure the beasts are adequately hydrated." He whistled for his steed, and Nimble followed behind it.

They continued at a more sensible walk toward the Weald, with Horra constantly glancing behind them. She stared unseeingly at the landscape around them. Too many thoughts jumbled in her mind to pay attention.

As the sun became a glowing ball, sinking into the horizon, the air thickened with magic. Not the heavy, dark kind of magic the Erlking wielded or the alluring magic of the fairies, but a light, invigorating magic. Lush, thick-trunked yew trees grew like sentries out of rich, loamy ground.

A voice spoke in her head. *"Welcome, Princess. You made it just in time."*

Horra dismounted Nimble and walked to the edge of the forest. She turned when Balk didn't follow. "Aren't you coming?"

He smiled. "I'm not sure what the voice told you, but it told me to wait here." He winked at her and motioned for her reins. "I'll keep Nimble safe."

She nodded, and taking a deep breath for courage, she grabbed her knapsack and entered the forest.

CHAPTER 42

Horra stepped into the forest and touched each of the yew trees. They grew in no certain order, and the space between them was narrow, leaving her only one path to take. Wind swished through the limbs.

The final yew tree was the largest by far. Glimmerbugs lit the branches and flittered in the air above an impressive garden. Saplings of different kinds grew out of the darkest soil Horra had ever seen.

A wizened old woodgoblin with a wooden cane hobbled up to her. He bowed. "Greetings, Princess Horra. I am Merrow, the seed keeper. Welcome to the Weald." His voice was deeper and more *clackity* than Woodsly's had been. He waved a branchlike arm toward the forest. "We have been intently waiting for you."

Horra took the seed from her pocket. She rubbed at the black spot. Was it larger than last time? She dropped it into the woodgoblin's eager limb. "I'm sorry for the delay."

He tipped his head. "I heard through the roots that you have had a harrowing adventure. But no matter. You've arrived just in time." Merrow turned the seed over in his hand. He clucked a sticklike, woodenish sound. Trees around him crackled and popped. "Dark magic indeed." He licked the seed and then spat something out. "A bit of poison as well. Good thing Woodsly was as powerful as he was and that you got here when you did. It might not have been viable for much longer."

A stone of doubt and worry grew in her gut. What if somehow, she'd allowed it to be destroyed? How could she live with herself if she failed her instructor?

Merrow's cane tapped across a rocky path, which extended in a pattern across the garden. It was the same symbol on her woodencloak. Shoving her anxiety aside, she pulled it out and studied it.

"Merrow, what does this symbol mean?" She pointed a claw at the cloak.

He glanced up from bending over a deep hole, which had already been dug in the ground. "It's a confound spell. Misdirects the viewer to see something that isn't there. Like a tree or a wall."

Merrow held the seed between his hands and spoke a prayer of thanksgiving and blessing over it. The seed lifted into the air and glowed brighter than the sun.

Horra covered her eyes. Hope bloomed again. It wouldn't light up if it didn't have life left, would it?

The seed dimmed and dropped back into Merrow's hands. He placed the seed in the hole. The bark on Merrow's face curled into a toothless smile. He took a bottle from a pouch belted to his pants and sprinkled something glittering over the seed. He dumped in some rich soil and then sprinkled more glittering substance into the hole. He repeated it until the hole was full.

Merrow patted the dome of dirt lovingly and smiled at Horra. "There. The consecration is done. Now we wait." He hobbled toward her. "I trust the woodencloak worked well for you?"

"It did, thank you. Do you need it back?" Horra folded the cloak into a neat square. Woodsly would be so proud of her. Her heart pinched.

Merrow shook his head. "You still need it, Princess. Your journey is far from over."

Horra's heart plunged. "But I thought my mission was to bring the seed to the Weald."

The woodgoblin stared hard at her. "It was and it wasn't."

When he made no move to speak further, Horra waited. She studied the pile of dirt. There was nothing special about it. Surely something should be happening? The glimmerbugs' lights flickered as they darted above them, lending blinking waves of light to the garden. She bided her time, fascinated at first, but growing impatient in the extended silence. "What will it be like? The seed? Will it be like Woodsly?"

Merrow turned to her. "Not as such, no. When a seed regenerates, it becomes a new creature. Odds are it will be nothing like my dear friend Woodsly."

"That's so sad," she whispered. Her throat tightened. She knew he was gone. But somehow this woodgoblin had made it more real. Heat washed across her face as she willed her tears away.

Merrow clacked out a laugh. "Woodsly confided in me that you often disappeared, hated doing your homework, and dawdled." He walked back to the mound. "He said you were adept but frustrating."

Horra's mouth hung open. Her tears dried up. "Wha—" she giggled. "I probably was an awful student."

He dropped a different red soil onto the mound and stared at it. "I assure you he was quite impressed by your work. Proud, even."

Her eyes heated again, and her nose ran from the threat of tears. She stopped it with her sleeve. "Thank you, I was never sure. Will it take long to grow?"

The woodgoblin sighed. He grabbed something hanging from one of the trees and returned to the spot where he'd planted the seed. "That is the quandary. It should be sprouting already. Gestationally, it will take a while for it to grow and then unroot."

Fear spun in her gut. She should've gotten here faster. "What do you mean it should already be sprouting? Is there something wrong?"

"The blight it suffered hinders its fertility." He added some sap to the soil. "Of course, you've suffered similar stifling magic and you broke through. Growth is a multi-faceted concept."

Growth? Horra stared at him. "I am short, but—"

"By unintentional accident, I'm afraid." He sprinkled some fizzy water on the mound. It bubbled and hissed.

Horra's pulse raced. She was confused. What accident was he referring to?

Merrow turned sharp, gray eyes her way. "Your mother's spoken wish at Norrow Lake was not her true wish. She desired for you to remain unchanged—innocent. Bitterness can twist a soul in untold ways—her truest fear for you. She knew there was no hope for remission. It had reached her heart, you see. She couldn't protect you from her death, but she tried to shield you from its consequences."

He gazed off into the distance. "The magic interpreted her request as best it could since her words and desires were conflicted. The combination of shrinking and growing broke the spell."

Horra's head spun. She always thought her mother's wish had failed to heal her. For three years she'd been mistaken. Magic hadn't failed her mother. Tears stung her eyes.

"It is hard to parse what is true, especially when it comes to magic. You, however, have overcome the force that bound your youth to you. And seeking forgiveness with the fairies is an important step for your emotional and spiritual growth." He pointed a stick finger at her. "Never forget that the Erlking didn't make that same choice. His path leads to destruction."

He scratched his head. "Might you have some of the expanding desserts with you now, Princess?"

"I believe so." She dug out the bag. There was only a meager amount of the giant's food left. "How do you know so much?"

"Trees communicate. Our root system spans all of the Wilden Lands. We are well-informed." He took the now-dried crumbs from her, crunched them in his stick hands, and sprinkled them over the soil. More sap went on top of that. The hole glowed a white-blue.

"Ah. Success!" Merrow's enthusiasm was catching.

Horra stepped closer to watch. Glimmerbugs darted furiously over them. Something vine-like poked out of the ground. It grew, sprouted a green leaf, and stopped.

Trees around them creaked and waved their limbs.

"Hmm. Strange, indeed." Merrow leaned over the hole. "Princess, would you happen to have more?"

She gave him what she had left.

Again, he sprinkled it over the hole, added the sap, and the light gleamed. The vine stretched and grew, becoming a sapling. Its smooth, brown bark was splotched with black spots.

"Will it be okay?"

"Only time will tell, but the seed is now viable. Hope survives. Thank you, Princess, for your part in keeping the balance of good and evil in our realm." He stepped away from the sapling and the glimmerbugs raced around it in a gleeful dance.

"Merrow, if you know all the things in the Wilden Lands, do you know who the Erlking is?" Horra hurried after him, her bare claws slapping against the smooth rock path.

He tapped his way along the narrow trail. "That I cannot say. His presence is like shifting shadows." Merrow shook his head. "There are some secrets even we don't know, Princess. What we have surmised is that there's a living malevolence that resides in the Riven Forest, a place we are repelled from. Our roots cannot breach the barrier. We need help. Because of this, your mission is not yet fulfilled."

Horra hugged the woodencloak to her chest. "What do I do next?"

Merrow pointed a stick finger in the air. "Return to your castle and get it back in order. The kingdoms must be united. And it is vital for Oddar to regain its standing and strength. We cannot allow the Erlking to reach his goal. We will send a messenger when the time comes for you to return here. Danger is ever-present. Guard the woodencloak with your life. It will serve you well." Merrow bowed and hobbled away. "Until we meet again, Princess."

Horra turned and made her way out of the Weald, the trees moving, making a path for her to walk. As she stepped out, it was as if she'd been asleep and had just woken, refreshed and ready. The sun was shining. It was morning already.

She found Balk sleeping against Nimble's side, his horse not far away. She kicked his boot. "Wake up. I have a new mission, and you have oaths to keep."

He grunted and rolled over. "Just another few minutes, Floke."

Should she douse him with water? She chose not to and settled against Nimble's warm, leathery side. She wanted to savor this brief triumph instead of racing off again. The air held just a hint of winter and the sun's golden glow was muted as well. She filled her lungs and slowly let the air out.

It wasn't just the season's change that quickened inside her bones. She had much to do when she returned to the castle. And for once, she was excited to see her father. She didn't dare examine his change of affection too closely. It was too fragile a thing. Besides, she might cry and she refused to do that again in front of the bocan who snored like the rattling of a mudpiper's call.

She prayed silently for her kingdom and the new druid that would unroot soon. If he was anything like Woodsly, he'd have the balance of good and evil in hand in short order.

Even though the Erlking had gotten away, for this brief moment in time, hope filled her. And she wouldn't trade that feeling for anything else in the Wilden Lands.

To Be Continued ...

ABOUT DAWN FORD

Winner of the 2016 ACFW Genesis Award and finalist in the 2018 Grace Award and the 2020 Great Expectations Contest, Dawn Ford has been recognized for her published and non-published works. Her flash fiction stories have been published in *Havok* magazine under both her real name and pen name, Jo Wonderly. Her debut novel, *Knee-high Lies*, was published in 2017.

As a child, Dawn often had her head in the clouds creating scenes and stories for anything and everything she came across. She believed there was magic everywhere, a sentiment she has never outgrown. Nature inspires her, and her love for the underdog and the unlikely hero colors much of what she writes.

Dawn adores anything Steampunk, is often distracted by shiny, pretty things, and her obsession with purses and shoes borders on hoarding. Dawn lives in Iowa and helps her husband run their foodservice and catering business out of Omaha, Nebraska. When not reading, writing, or catering, Dawn loves babysitting her grandchildren, is parent to Snickers the Wonder Beagle, and can usually be caught daydreaming.

The Girl with Stars in Her Eyes

Firebird Series—Book One

Eighteen-year-old servant girl Tambrynn is haunted by more than her unusual silver hair and the star-shaped pupils in her eyes. Her uncontrollable ability to call objects leads the wolves who savagely murdered her mother right to her door.

When she's fired and outcast during a snowstorm, her carriage wrecks and she's forced to find refuge in an abandoned cottage. There, her life is upended when the magpie who's stalked her for ten years transforms into a man, Lucas. He's her Watcher and they're from a different kingdom. His job is to keep her safe from her father, an evil mage, who wants to steal her abilities, turn her into one of his undead beasts, and become immortal himself.

Can they make it to the magical passageway and get to their home kingdom in time for Tambrynn to thwart her father's malicious plans? Or will Tambrynn's unique magic doom them all?

Get your copy here:

https://scrivenings.link/thegirlwithstarsinhereyes

The Girl with Fire in Her Veins

Firebird Series—Book Two

Former servant girl Tambrynn struggles with her new firebird abilities, especially the internal fire she cannot control. So, she, along with her Watcher Lucas, and her grandfather Bennett journey to a hidden mountain keep to find the answers she seeks before she sets the kingdom aflame.

But there's a new dragon who's targeting Tambrynn, a mergirl who wishes to manipulate her, and the froggen king, Siltworth, who hasn't forgotten that Tambrynn destroyed his watery reign. When her father, the evil mage Thoron, attacks someone she loves, Tambrynn's group is separated and she has to face another powerful foe alone.

Is she strong enough to withstand the deluge? Or will she drown in the fire and the flood?

Available April 25, 2023:

https://scrivenings.link/thegirlwithfireinherveins

The Whisperer's Wish

by Janilise Lloyd

For sixteen years, Laurelin Moore has been keeping a secret. She is a whisperer, and she knows that to reveal her gift now is a dangerous risk. Past whisperers have been exploited for their power. But Ausland's queen is dead and acknowledging her magic is her only chance at becoming a Rook in the Pentax—a competition that will decide the kingdom's next ruler.

Laurelin isn't in it for the crown, though. She's after the wish that will be granted to the victor. A wish that would save her dying brother, Pippin. But there are dangerous undercurrents to the competition, and Laurelin finds herself at the center of it. She begins to search for answers and discovers a secret with the potential to shatter the entire kingdom.

Coming March 21, 2023

https://scrivenings.link/thewhispererswish

Beyond the Gates by Erin R. Howard

Gates of Deceit—Book One

If playing by the rules means it keeps you alive, then seventeen-year-old Renna James should know better. She is, after all, the one who broadcasts these rules to the Outpost. What lies beyond the gates had always lured her, but her venture outside wasn't supposed to leave her locked out. Now, Renna's one chance to survive the next seventy-two hours just ran into the forest she's forbidden to enter.

Get your copy here:

https://scrivenings.link/beyondthegates

Kokopelli's Song

Book One of the Four Corners Fantasy Series

When seventeen-year-old Amy Adams finds her father's family and a lost twin brother on the Hopi reservation in Arizona, she stumbles into a struggle between shamans and witches that spans a thousand years. After Mahu is attacked and a Conquistador's journal stolen, Amy and her new friend Diego set out on a dangerous quest to find and perform the ceremony that can stop ancient evil from entering our world.

But Amy and Diego are not alone as they race against time measured by a waxing moon. Kokopelli's song, the haunting notes of a red cedar flute, guides them along the migration route sacred to pueblo peoples: West to Old Oraibi, South to El Morro, East to Cochiti Pueblo, North to Chimney Rock, and finally to the Center—and the final confrontation—in Chaco Canyon.

Get your copy here:

https://scrivenings.link/kokopellissong

ExpanseBooks.pub and ScrivKids.com are imprints of Scrivenings Press LLC.

Stay up-to-date on your favorite books and authors with our free e-newsletters.

https://scriveningspress.com/newsletter-signup/

www.ingramcontent.com/pod-product-compliance
Lightning Source LLC
Chambersburg PA
CBHW070631100726
47907CB00007B/1932